Vice & Virtue

Wooldridges. $16.95

Books by the same author

Angelmonster
The Boy-Free Zone
Cassandra's Sister
Fish Feet
Monkey
Shakespeare's Apprentice

For younger readers

Dandelion and Bobcat
The *Poppy Love* series

Vice & Virtue

VERONICA BENNETT

**WALKER
BOOKS**

First published in Great Britain 2011 by Walker Books Ltd
87 Vauxhall Walk, London SE11 5HJ

2 4 6 8 10 9 7 5 3 1

Text © 2011 Veronica Bennett
Cover design © 2011 Walker Books Ltd

This book has been typeset in Bembo

Printed and bound in Great Britain by Clays Ltd, St Ives plc

British Library Cataloguing in Publication Data:
a catalogue record for this book is
available from the British Library

ISBN 978-1-4063-1140-2

www.walker.co.uk

London 1700: The World of *Vice and Virtue*

In 1700 the people of England were recovering from one of the most unsettled periods in their history. The Civil War of the 1640s had resulted in the beheading of King Charles I and an eleven-year period of republican rule, first under Oliver Cromwell and, later, his son Richard. The monarchy had been restored when Charles II ascended the throne in 1660, but in 1688 his Catholic successor, James II, had been deposed by anti-Catholic activists in the "Glorious Revolution", and the throne taken by the Protestant William of Orange and his wife, King James's daughter, Mary.

When this story opens, King William was a widower, Queen Mary having died in 1694. There was still great hostility between Catholics and Protestants and society was racked by corruption and distrust. No one, however wealthy or influential, was safe in a world where intrigue was a way of life. And nowhere was this more evident than in London. By far the largest city in England, it was so crowded and unregulated that anyone, should they so desire, could slip away, disappear down a back street and become someone else.

A Powder Keg

The man was watching her.

She turned away, but when she looked back he was still looking at her. She was sure she had never seen him before, though she and her mother and sisters came often to stroll and watch the people in St James's Park, surrounded by crowds doing the same thing. Who was to say how long he had been standing there, watching?

"Aurora, are you listening?"

"No." Aurora did not look at her mother, but kept her eyes on the man. "I am wondering what interest that man can possibly have in me."

"Where?" Mrs Eversedge followed Aurora's gaze. "Point him out."

"She cannot do that without letting him see we are speaking of him," observed Flora.

"What does that matter?" Mrs Eversedge took Aurora's arm. "Now tell me, which is he?"

As discreetly as possible, Aurora indicated the gentleman, who stood with another gentleman beside the park gate. Both men were well dressed, one taller than the other, each wearing a sword, a wig and a three-cornered hat.

"The tall one or the short one?" asked Eleanora.

"The short one."

"Oh! The other looks much better-favoured."

"Well, *he* is not the one who was staring at me." Aurora was beginning to weary of this. She wished to get out of the man's sight and go home.

"Are you sure he was not looking at *me*?" said Flora.

"Which one? The tall one or the short one?" asked Eleanora again.

"Oh, be quiet, girls!" Mrs Eversedge was as disappointed as her daughters that Aurora had aroused the interest of the less handsome gentleman. "It is time we turned, anyway. The sun is going."

It had been the kind of spring afternoon that transformed the park into a scene glittering not only with natural beauty, but with silks, jewels, swords, buckles and the polished harnesses of horses. Now the receding sunlight threw long shadows across the lawns, making Aurora and her sisters look taller than they really were. Perhaps, she thought as they turned homeward, the shorter man's shadow was doing the same for him.

She did not listen to Flora and Eleanora's chatter. The late afternoon contained much to enjoy. A breeze brushed her cheeks, bringing the mingled scents of blossom trees and grass clippings. Beyond the park gates, these gave way to the familiar street odours of horse dung, gutter slops, chimney smoke.

London, thought Aurora, city of dreams.

What dreams did it hold for her? Marriage to a rich man? It was unlikely. Girls like the Eversedge sisters, whose only contact with genteel society came during these promenades in St James's Park, had nothing but their beauty to recommend them to suitors.

She sighed inwardly. When she was young, younger even than thirteen-year-old Eleanora, she *had* dreamed of standing beside a handsome man at the altar of St Margaret's Church, where her own parents had been married. But that was before Father had caught a cold, which turned to a putrid throat, which turned to a fever. Within four days of his first sneeze they had laid him in the ground. Within three days of *that*, they had been turned out of their house by the landlord, to whom Father had been in debt for six months' rent, and obliged to take lodgings in Billingsgate, near the fish market.

On their first day there, they had gathered despondently round the dinner table. "Well, girls," Mrs Eversedge had said briskly as she served the food – yes, fish – "I must provide for you now, by doing what I do best."

"Which is what?" ten-year-old Flora had asked.

"Who made that pinafore you have on?" demanded her mother. "And smocked the front, and embroidered the hem?"

"But you cannot be a seamstress!" Flora had protested. "What would Father—"

"Not a *seamstress*," said Mrs Eversedge, setting down the last dish in her own place. "I shall advertise myself as a mantua-maker, which is altogether a different thing."

Aurora was anxious at first. True, wealthy ladies would always need new gowns, and mantua-making was a respectable profession for a widow. But Mrs Eversedge had no shop, no professional reputation and very few connections. Business was slow, and she was obliged to sew shirts and nightclothes as well as the elaborate petticoats, cloaks, bodices and over-gowns ordered by her customers. She got up early and stayed up late, going about her work with a zeal twelve-year-old Aurora marvelled at every day. She got thinner – they all did – but as time went by, their mother's skill and energy brought her more and more commissions.

Five years had passed since then. The Eversedges now lived in a house rented from a respectable landlord in Dacre Street, near Westminster Abbey. Each girl had been tutored in her letters and numbers, and taught to sew and keep house. Their mother had many loyal customers for her gowns, and she also sold material, ribbons, silks and thread from her shop on the ground floor. Proudly, she told friends that from her display of *feminine* wares (Aurora, Flora and Eleanora themselves), any man of substance would be pleased to choose a wife.

"Shall we go to the park tomorrow?"

Flora was waiting at the shop door, her weight on one foot while she tapped the other on the step, her round face full of expectation.

"Why not?" said Aurora. She liked the park; if the man was not there, no matter.

"What shall you wear?" asked Eleanora.

"Shush, girls." Mrs Eversedge was searching her pocket for her keys. "It does not signify what Aurora wears. His friend was much better-looking, anyway."

The better-looking friend, Aurora knew, was part of Flora's determination to revisit the park. Though only fifteen, Flora considered herself prettier than either of her sisters and was determined to get to the altar before Aurora, who was two years older. For Aurora's part, she thought Flora's face too wide, and secretly suspected that Eleanora would turn out to be the superior beauty.

"I shall sponge and press my blue gown," she told her sister. "And you, Flora dear, may dress my hair."

But there was no need for them to go back to the park. Before Aurora had finished dressing the next morning, she heard excited yelping on the stairs, and her mother threw open the bedroom door, thrust a piece of folded paper into Aurora's hand and stood back in satisfaction.

"There!" she cried. "He has brought you that note! And he is waiting downstairs!"

Aurora was so astonished that she dropped both the paper and the petticoat she had been about to put on. She bent down, took the note from the rumpled material and broke the seal.

Hartford House, Islington
April 22nd, 1700

Dear Miss_____

I beg your indulgence of such an unseemly form of address, but I do not know your name. I know you only as the lady I chanced to see some weeks ago in St James's Park, walking with a feminine party I would guess to consist of your mother and sisters. Since then I have returned to the park daily in the hope of seeing you again. Have you noticed my interest in you, I wonder? If so, please forgive me, but I was entranced.

In vain I have asked if any of my acquaintance knows you; I have tried by various means to secure your name and the whereabouts of your house. But I am afraid that by yesterday afternoon my patience was exhausted, and I resorted to low tactics. My friend and I followed you (discreetly, I believe; you did not see us) and noted which house you and your family entered. This morning I have returned, bearing this note.

I will be waiting, by your mother's good grace, for a reply. If you wish to dismiss me, please add your wishes to this note and return it to me by your housemaid's hand. If you would condescend – and I desire this most passionately – to meet me, I am at your service.

Yours in hope,
Edward Francis

Aurora looked up to find herself surrounded by three expectant faces.

"What does he say?" asked Eleanora.

"Make haste and get dressed!" Mrs Eversedge pulled Aurora's arm. "Hester!" she called to the maid. "Bring Miss Aurora's blue gown!"

"Does he mention his friend?" asked Flora.

"Actually, he does." Aurora handed her the letter. "And he mentions you, too, though not in the context you might hope. Here, take it. I do not know what to do with it. It is a powder keg."

"What do you mean, a powder keg?" asked Eleanora. "You do say some odd things sometimes, Aurora."

Aurora stepped into her petticoat and drew it around her waist. "I mean that this piece of paper contains something that might burn my fingers. If I agree to meet this gentleman, who can tell where it will lead?"

Flora was snorting in disbelief as she read. "Gentleman! I would wager that he is *not* a gentleman, and wishes merely to—"

"Flora! He *is* a gentleman, and a wealthy one, by the look of him," insisted her mother. "I want no foolishness from any of you girls."

"Do you think he wishes to *marry* Aurora?" asked Eleanora.

"Of course not," snapped Flora.

"But supposing he does?" persisted her sister.

"Then she must decide upon her answer." Mrs Eversedge looked at Aurora calmly. "And she had better be quick about it, in case he should change his mind. Hester, show the gentleman into the parlour."

Ten minutes later, Aurora followed her mother downstairs to the parlour door. She concentrated on counting the frills on the back of Mrs Eversedge's second-best cap, trying to control the shaking of her legs beneath her skirt and the shortness of her breath beneath her blue silk bodice.

Her mother paused with her hand on the doorknob. "Remember, child…"

"Decide quickly," recited Aurora. "In case he should change his mind."

Edward Francis was standing by the window. The light of the April morning fell on his slight figure, illuminating the hollows of his face beneath his wig. Aurora and her mother curtseyed low as he turned. "We are honoured, Mr Francis," said Mrs Eversedge. "I am Catherine Eversedge. May I present my daughter, Miss Aurora Eversedge?"

The gentleman executed an awkward bow. The thought passed through Aurora's head that he was embarrassed. Or perhaps, now that he had inspected her more closely, he was regretting his impulsiveness.

"The honour is all mine." His voice was quiet and cultured. A little effeminate, Aurora decided. And she did not like his green suit, nor his green hat. Green was an unlucky colour.

Propriety demanded that a mother chaperone her daughter in such situations, but Mrs Eversedge knew when to treat propriety with circumspection. Pleading her duties to two other girls who awaited her upstairs, she curtseyed to Mr Francis, gave Aurora a meaningful glance and quitted the room. Aurora sat down and gestured for Mr Francis to do the same. He sat on a straight-backed chair, arranging the skirt of his coat and adjusting his elaborately decorated cuffs. As he did so, she had leisure to look at him.

She had always pictured the man who came to court her as tall – taller than her father, and at least as strong. He would be a horseman and a swordsman. And he would be rich, of course. But the only aspect of this picture presented by Edward Francis was the last. Wealth he might have, but he had no bearing. Neither his height nor his breadth spoke of a man of action. He carried a sword, as all gentlemen did, but Aurora doubted he knew how to use it.

His shoulders were narrow, and so rounded that he walked with a stoop. His face, though not positively ugly, was plain. Thick eyebrows lay in straight lines above eyes so dark that Aurora could not tell where the pupil ended and the iris began. And it was a lean, bony face. The man looked, for all his wealth, as if he did not get enough to eat.

"Your mother understands the nature of my visit, Miss Eversedge?" he said.

"Yes, sir," said Aurora.

The room was very hot; there was perspiration on the

back of Aurora's neck, under the tendrils of her lower hair, which Flora had dressed fashionably over her shoulders. The rest of her hair, swept into a topknot secured with satin ribbons, felt as if it would tumble if she moved her head. She wondered if the necessity of keeping still made her look elegant, or merely ridiculous.

"Do *you* understand it?" he asked her.

"I believe so, sir."

Some of the tension left his face, though his expression was still apprehensive. "Then God has smiled upon me. I feared that you would dismiss me as a charlatan, or a philanderer. But I swear I am in earnest."

He looked to her for encouragement.

"Very well, sir," she said.

"I do not presume," he continued, "to fathom your reasons for allowing me into your company. I can only describe my own motive for resorting to this unorthodox method of approaching a young lady. When I saw you in the park, something happened to me which I had despaired of ever happening."

Aurora lowered her eyelids modestly.

"Miss Eversedge, I have no doubt that you are the woman I love. And if you have any compassion in your soul, I implore you, consider my situation."

She looked up, surprised by the speed of his declaration. His black eyes did not blink; his lips were unsmiling. There was nothing in his countenance to suggest a man in love.

He settled himself more comfortably in his chair. "My father, who is recently deceased, wished me to do something that he himself did, many years ago, and which gave him happiness for much of his life. He wished me to marry for love." All the while he was speaking, he brushed imaginary dust from his breeches. "Of course, if I were to fall in love with a woman of means, from a wealthy family who would bestow upon her a sizeable dowry, so much the better. I have tried my best to secure such a match. I have been introduced to Lady This and Miss That, and their sisters. Widows and fortune-hunters have pursued me, or rather my wealth. Unfortunately, not one of these ladies possesses what I am searching for."

He paused, his eyebrows drawn together. Then his watchful eyes again fell on Aurora's face. "Miss Eversedge, my feelings are strong, and utterly sincere."

"Sir—" she began, but found herself silenced.

"You are not only beautiful, but you are graceful. You wear your simple gowns with more elegance than the daughter of an earl, and yet with a pleasing lack of vanity. And now that we have been introduced, I find the sweetness of your voice very much to my liking."

Aurora accepted his compliments in silence, bowing her head as low as the insecure topknot allowed.

"I understand this is very sudden," he added, "since we have only just met."

Aurora remained silent. He seemed encouraged by this; she heard him take in breath in preparation for his next words.

"Miss Eversedge, if you will consent, I very much desire to make you my wife." All apprehension was gone from his voice. "But under a condition you must allow me to enforce."

Aurora felt very hot. Her heart thudded, sending blood rushing to her face and neck. She sat on the edge of the chair, her words to Eleanora repeating themselves in her brain. It was clear now that she truly was embarking on something as unpredictable, and potentially as damaging, as setting a flame to a barrel of gunpowder. Could she really agree to marry a man unknown to her and her family, merely because he requested it, and her mother encouraged it?

She wished she had the courage to rise, make a curtsey, tell Mr Francis she was grateful for his offer but must refuse it, and leave the room. But she was not courageous, and her mother had to find *three* men who would take her daughters without a marriage portion. That a wealthy man should present himself with no effort on anyone's part was a stroke of fortune not to be dismissed.

"What is the condition, sir?" she asked.

"That the wedding be a clandestine one, conducted in one of the so-called chapels near the Fleet river."

Aurora stared at him. Aware that her mouth had fallen open, she closed it and tried to collect herself. "What can possibly be the need for such a condition, sir?"

His thin lips stretched into a humourless smile. "Perhaps you will understand better if I tell you that I am in ill health." He rested his head on the back of the chair, slightly dislodging his wig. Aurora caught a glimpse of dark hair, choppily cut above his ears. His thin features and stooping frame made it difficult to estimate his years, but she hoped the wig did not cover a prematurely bald pate. "I have consumption," he said bleakly.

For the first time, Aurora was moved. His story of his search for a bride had been as commonplace as his appearance was plain. But that he was suffering from an illness that always ended in an agonizing death was truly tragic.

"Perhaps," he went on, "you have been given a clue by my appearance. I am thin and pale, I know. I live in Islington for the fresh air, but I cannot follow country pursuits. Nor do I attend social functions. I have a large library, and still play the violin when I have sufficient energy."

Aurora's spirits sank. First the demand that her wedding be unacknowledged by society, now the news that if she married Edward Francis no hunting parties, no balls, no visitors and no outings awaited her. "So am I to take it that a clandestine wedding is necessitated by … a shortage of time?"

He did not look at her. She saw his throat work as he swallowed repeatedly. He must have planned his answer to this inevitable question, but he was uncomfortable nonetheless. Some time passed while he considered.

Aurora waited. The sunrays had travelled while they had been talking and now fell upon Edward Francis's shoulders, making the green of his coat greener. At last his eyes, so black they seemed neither to absorb nor reflect light, turned their flat gaze towards her. He spoke softly.

"You are quite correct. I do not have much time left on this earth. I cannot wait for the banns to be read and the period required by the law to expire. Furthermore, in view of your family circumstances, we shall not be delayed by the drawing-up of a financial contract. If you are willing, we can be married next week."

Aurora contemplated him steadily. She could not warm to the man, but she was impressed by his candour. And although his declaration of love had not moved her, without doubt it had flattered her.

"After my death," he continued, "my lands and fortune will be bequeathed to you and, if we are so blessed, my son or daughter. I am my parents' only child, Miss Eversedge. I long for an heir."

Into Aurora's brain floated the often-imagined picture of herself and a tall, strong man kneeling at the altar of St Margaret's, beneath a radiant east window. She sat silently, her hands in her lap, contemplating the pale face of the man before her. A man old before his time, weighed down by illness and strain.

"Mr Francis," she said at last. "I know I am free to refuse you. If I do, may I have your word that no part of what has passed between us today will ever escape your lips?"

He nodded, keeping his eyes on her face. "Upon my honour, you do, madam."

"The choice is mine?"

He nodded again. Aurora felt the colour come again into her cheeks, but she kept her expression calm. "Then may I ask, sir, on what basis your choice of me as the woman you wish to marry is based? Apart from physical attraction, that is?"

He had not expected this. His countenance clouded; he cast his glance downwards, and was silent for a few moments, preparing his words. Then he raised his eyes, which regarded her with an apologetic, almost sheepish expression. "Miss Eversedge, you have just given me confirmation, if any were needed, of the prudence and intelligence I suspected you possess. You will commit yourself to nothing until you are satisfied that I am not intent upon villainy, and quite right." He gave a shallow sigh.

"I confess, I have not been entirely truthful. I did not address you in my letter by your name, but the fact is, I already knew it."

His eyes continued to hold her gaze. He was embarrassed, but not, as far as Aurora could discern, humbled by his confession.

"Why did you not use it, then, sir?" she asked.

"I considered it. But I decided you would be more likely to hear me out if I met you first and explained my circumstances in person, before allowing you to know that my selection was not as random as I have implied."

Aurora digested this. It sounded plausible. If the letter had begun "Dear Miss Eversedge", her first thought would have been that Edward Francis had vaulted several social barriers in one leap, not only following her home but addressing her by name when they had not been introduced. It was true, she would have thought the less of him, and his manners.

"I understand, sir," she told him warily. "But pray tell me, how did you know who I am?"

He was still looking at her steadily, but now his eyes took on a sharper look. "Because I knew your late father, William Eversedge."

Aurora's surprise must have shown on her face, because Edward Francis smiled sympathetically. "I am sorry to astonish you so, but the truth is, both my own late father and myself were associates of him and his friends, and share his…" He paused, searching Aurora's face for recognition of what he was about to say.

She gave it without hesitation. "His loyalties?"

"Indeed. I too am loyal to King William, and I am persuaded you are also."

"I am, sir," Aurora assured him. "The King may be the Defender of the Protestant Faith, Mr Francis, but be in no doubt that I am equally unshakeable in my defence of it. King James shall never again sit upon the throne of England!"

He smiled. "You are your father's daughter, I see." His tone was mild, but there was conviction in it. "When I saw your mother, whom I recognized as William Eversedge's widow, can you blame me for taking special notice of her eldest daughter? Quite apart from your obvious charms, I knew you would share the convictions my father passed to me. And so would any heir you and I might be fortunate enough to have."

Aurora considered. Sincere-sounding though this speech was, she was not seduced by it. She had been given the explanation she had asked for, and now all that remained was for her to make her decision. Nothing had changed in the last few minutes; her choice was still a stark one: between marriage to a man she did not know, and certainly did not love, and the rejection of money, status and family connections she may never have another chance to obtain.

She surveyed him carefully as he sat in the chair. His green suit, his pale countenance, his over-decorated cuffs, his pedagogic air – nothing about him attracted her. Was she about to agree to marry this stranger because she would be a fool not to? She had never considered herself mercenary, and had often been uneasy at the casual dismissal of love in favour of fortune that marriage seemed to demand. But now she had been given the opportunity to make a stand against the prevailing attitude, would she do so, or not?

Yesterday, her future had seemed certain, lying before

her as plain as a map. She would continue to live in the amiable but restrictive household at Dacre Street, under her mother's command. She and her sisters would do what they could to secure the attentions of, perhaps, an under-clerk, a hatter, or, if one of them were extremely fortunate, a young clergyman hopeful of employment as soon as a living became available.

If Aurora had been a man, she would have been able to express her interest in the daily turmoil of London life, from the activities of Parliament and the court to the latest satirical play. She would have been able to frequent coffee houses, immersing herself in political gossip, being amused by the fearlessness of young plotters and agitators, discussing the contents of pamphlets and journals with other like-minded supporters of the king.

But because she had been born female, she could do none of these things. Certainly, she had read every one of her father's books, many of them more than once, and she read the news; she knew what was happening in the world. But Mrs Eversedge's social circle did not include educated people who brought their intellect to bear on the questions of the day. Aurora was forced to accompany her on calls, sitting for hours in cramped parlours, stifled by both the lack of air and the banality of the conversation. And dreaming of escape from the world of women.

But today, her future was no longer certain. Freedom beckoned. Though it might come at a price Aurora could not predict, the powder keg was ready for her to ignite the fuse. She would have the freedom to be mistress of her own house, to wear fine clothes, and speak of politics with concerned men who were prepared to hear her opinions.

And then, later, to be a rich widow, perhaps the mother of a son or daughter, and to be able to choose her second husband from a stream of suitors. What an extraordinary luxury for the daughter of a mantua-maker!

Her heart thudded. Ignoring the whispering of her conscience, she extended her hand. "I thank you for your offer, Mr Francis," she said, endeavouring to keep her voice steady, "and I have made my decision. I *will* marry you. I accept your condition of a clandestine marriage, and I will do my best to be a good wife."

"My dear Miss Eversedge. Aurora..." He rose, bowed and kissed her fingers lightly. "You have made me the happiest of men."

Aurora did not wish to contemplate her own conduct. She stood up, no longer looking at him. "Since I am but seventeen years old, sir, you must ask permission of my mother. If you will excuse me, I will fetch her now."

He nodded. "Will you not shake my hand?"

The shadows beneath his eyes were deep, but Aurora no longer felt pity. He had secured the potential means of obtaining an heir before it was too late, and she had secured her escape from Dacre Street. "Yes, I will shake your hand," she said. "We have made a bargain, after all."

He took her outstretched fingers. His hand was scarcely bigger then Aurora's own, with narrow fingers and well-tended nails. "Indeed we have, Miss Eversedge," he replied without animation. "Indeed we have."

A Garter on His Hat

Aurora plunged her nose into the scented handkerchief in her left hand. Her right hand held a bouquet, which would have served equally well to mask the stink of the river. But she did not want to use it as a nosegay. It was her wedding bouquet.

"For all that this river is called the Fleet, it is *not* very fleet," observed Flora. "It hardly runs at all."

"And it smells to heaven!" added Eleanora. "You had better hurry and get married, Aurora, so that we may escape from this unholy stench."

"I cannot marry until my groom arrives," replied Aurora.

"What will you do if he does not come?"

"He *will* come," insisted her mother. "And by God's grace, you and Flora too will come to be married in this place soon enough, stink or no stink."

Eleanora pouted and looked with disapproval at the inn sign above their heads. "I shall not be married *here*!" she declared. "My husband will stand beside me at the altar of Westminster Abbey itself!"

"You wish to marry the bishop, then?" suggested Flora, with a sideways look at Aurora.

"Not at all, you simpleton…" Eleanora caught the look. "Do not tease me!"

Aurora too might have wished to be married in the sight of God, rather than in a plainly furnished room behind an inn, the ceremony presided over by a parson long since disgraced. She would rather have had the luxury of the time afforded by the reading of the banns in which to choose a length of fashionable material and have her mother make a beautiful wedding dress. But however much she had considered the situation during the seven days and nights that had passed since Mr Francis's proposal, she could find nothing actually illogical in his request for a hasty wedding. They must marry now, and Aurora must be satisfied with only one item of new finery – a wide-brimmed hat, lavishly trimmed with flowers by the excited fingers of Flora and Eleanora. Apart from that, her blue dress and best gloves would suffice until such time as she could employ her own dressmaker and milliner, and visit the glover, hosier and shoemaker whenever she wished. In short, when she was Mrs Edward Francis, a woman of means.

She knew she should be happy that such a rich man wished to marry her, under any circumstances. But she did not feel happy. She felt perplexed, unsettled and disappointed.

"Something is happening over there," declared Flora, craning her neck. "Could that be Mr Francis and his groomsman?"

A carriage had been prevented from coming nearer than the end of the street by the narrowness of the space between the jutting upper storeys. Two men emerged from its door, one tall and fair-faced, the other smaller and stooping.

"Aye, that is my would-be husband," observed Aurora without enthusiasm. "And the man he was with in the park."

Flora bounced a little on her toes. "The tall one is—"

"I know, the better-looking," said Aurora. "You will have to set your cap at him, Flora. I am sure you know how."

The gloom of the street was too great for Aurora to see Mr Francis's features distinctly, but his wiry frame and round shoulders were unmistakeable. He was wearing another highly decorated jacket, dark red this time, and a long wig. His sword hung at his left side, but, unlike his companion, he did not rest his hand upon it as he approached. His right hand held a walking-stick, which he leaned on with every step.

Aurora's heart contracted with pity. If his condition had so weakened him within a single week, how many weeks could she expect to pass before she became a widow? Silently, she prayed. *If it please you, God, allow Mr Francis to live long enough for me to bear him an heir, and give his father happiness beyond the grave. This I ask you from my heart. Amen.*

"My deepest and most humble apologies for keeping you waiting," Mr Francis said to the ladies with a bow, "but I found myself indisposed this morning and had to take a little time to recover." His friend went to his side, ready to support him if he staggered, but Mr Francis waved him away. His eyes beneath the curled wig alighted upon Aurora. "I am quite well now," he said softly, "and happier than I have ever been."

Aurora knew she had turned pink. She curtseyed. "I am honoured, Mr Francis."

"Please, you must call me Edward. And so must all your family."

The other ladies curtseyed, Flora and Eleanora unable to resist a giggling glance at one another. "Thank you, Edward," said Mrs Eversedge.

"And this is my good friend and groomsman, Richard Allcott. Richard, allow me to introduce Mrs Catherine Eversedge and her daughters Miss Aurora, Miss Flora and Miss Eleanora Eversedge."

They curtseyed; Mr Allcott bowed, ignoring the quizzical look thrown at him by Flora. "Delighted," he said and, with a glance at Edward, he opened the door of the inn and offered his arm to Mrs Eversedge. "Madam, shall we enter?"

The innkeeper ushered them into a low-ceilinged room with a small window and a bare floor. Behind an oak table was a carved chair, and before it stood two plain chairs with shabby worked cushions. Aurora wondered how many hopeful, or apprehensive, or relieved, or possibly happy men and women had sat on those cushions.

An elderly man in the black garb of a clergyman appeared through a doorway behind the table. He indicated the assortment of benches arranged around the room, then patted the cushion on the left-hand chair. "The bride is to sit here, and the groom on the other chair, if you please."

They sat down. Edward reached into his pocket and laid some coins upon the Prayer Book on the table, and the ceremony began. Before many minutes had passed, Aurora and Edward had each made their responses, and Edward had placed a gold ring upon Aurora's finger.

Within another few minutes the clergyman had presented certificates for them to sign, and in less than a minute after that, they were pronounced married.

"Your names shall be entered in the parish register without delay," the clergyman informed them. And with that, he opened the door behind the table and disappeared.

Aurora was trembling. It was too late to go back now. She had done it. She was married. Her ears buzzed. All she could hear was her mother sniffling into a handkerchief.

She felt Edward take her arm. "The wedding breakfast awaits us at Hartford House," he announced to the company. "Come, my wife and I will lead the way."

Aurora got to her feet, and the little wedding party walked out of the mean room, through the inn and into the street. All around them strangers noticed their smart clothes and Aurora's bouquet, and called out good wishes.

The carriage was still at the end of the street. Edward's coachman, who looked no older than Aurora herself, handed the ladies to their seats. Then he took Edward's stick, settled him comfortably and placed a rug around his knees. "Thank you, Burns," said his master.

The carriage swayed as Burns and Richard Allcott climbed up to the box. Aurora heard a shouted command to the horses, then the creaking of the wheels. Their progress over the cobbles was slow and jolting. She looked out of the window, wondering how long it would be before she saw London streets again.

She shifted her gaze. Her husband, who sat opposite, was watching her, smiling. There it was, the thin-lipped smile that barely creased the corners of his mouth, studied and self-conscious. Aurora did not return it.

* * *

The wedding breakfast continued into the late afternoon. In a dining room from which long windows opened on to a pretty garden, Aurora's sisters had fallen upon a table spread with cold beef, pies, sweetmeats, cheese, fruit and the kind of wine jellies they had last seen before their father died, and then only at Christmas. But Aurora had not allowed herself to feel embarrassed. It was clear that Edward Francis had no intention of displaying anything but generosity towards her relations; she had resolved to let his behaviour be the guide of hers.

As dusk spread over the garden, she watched a man-servant lighting the wall candles. Fatigue, wine and rich food had rendered her very sleepy. She put her elbows on the table, supported her chin on her hands and endeavoured to keep her eyes from closing.

"Aurora!" Flora, her round face pink with excitement, seized both her sister's hands and tried to draw her to her feet. "Come on, the dancing is beginning! And you know what the gentlemen must do! Mother, you tell her!"

Mrs Eversedge regarded her eldest daughter with affection. "You are tired, my dear, I know, but tradition must play its part."

Aurora rose unsteadily. A group of musicians waited in the corner of the room while the man-servant and the young coachman moved the table nearer the wall to make space for dancing. Feeling foolish, she curtseyed to Edward, and he bowed. Both he and Richard Allcott, who was bowing to Flora, were smiling, though Edward's unease was obvious.

Aurora sympathized with him. She knew she had to be

patient with her sisters' enthusiasm for wedding tradition. But a man whose lungs were diseased would surely dance only the first, and Mr Allcott was the only other gentleman present. If they wished to dance for longer, Aurora and her sisters, not for the first time, would have to partner each other.

The dancing began. The musicians played a stately court dance rather than a country jig, for Edward's benefit. Richard Allcott's task as groomsman would have been easier if the music had been fast enough to require the holding-up of skirts. But he was determined to perform the ritual regardless. Clearing his throat, he spoke to Aurora in a voice loud enough to be heard above the music as he led Flora round. "You will give me your garter as a marriage token, will you not, my lady?"

In the shadow of his hat brim Aurora saw the expression in his eyes: amused, but determined. She turned away her face, pretending bashfulness, and took a few more measures with Edward. "Sir, you are impertinent!" she scolded Mr Allcott.

Flora, more delighted by the playing-out of this scene than the prospect of more dancing, let go of her partner's hand. "Go on, Mr Allcott!" she whispered urgently. "We have tied the garter low for you!"

"Impertinent? Never!" declared Richard Allcott gravely. "Gallant? Certainly!"

Aurora released Edward's hand and looked at the faces of her sisters. Each was pink-cheeked from wine and bright-eyed from excitement, and over each was spread a joyful abandon she had not seen there in years. The attentiveness of Edward and his friend, clearly intended to make up for the shortcomings of the wedding, had turned

Flora and Eleanora for the moment into young girls newly out of childhood, without anxiety and eager for innocent entertainment. Which, of course, they should be. How Aurora wished they could remain so!

"What will you do, sir?" she asked Mr Allcott, who looked so comically solemn she could hardly keep her countenance.

"Why, steal it!"

The musicians began a fast tune. Amid squeals from her sisters, Aurora set off around the room, followed by Richard Allcott, who repeatedly lunged towards her, trying to lift the hem of her gown. She pleased the onlookers by turning round and round, holding down her skirts against her pursuer's attempts to raise them. As the room whirled around her, she was aware of Edward, resting on a chair, watching her.

She was unwary for a second, and immediately Mr Allcott reached under her skirt as far as the white silk garter below her right knee. It untied as he pulled it. With a yelp of triumph, he twirled it round above his head, then tied it round his hat.

"Do I not look fine?" he asked, placing his hand on his sword and striding around the room like a dandy.

"Very fine indeed," said Edward from his chair. "Will you steal the other garter, and fasten it to *my* hat?"

Aurora, her eyes on Edward's face, allowed Mr Allcott to lift the hem of her skirt again. While the garter was being retrieved, she and Edward continued to look at each other. Several times today she had tried, unsuccessfully, to fathom his expression. This time was no different. She saw that he was entertained by the spectacle, though his face held some of the bemused embarrassment it had shown earlier. But she could not read the meaning of the flash of emotion that crossed his countenance when he grasped the piece of white silk Mr Allcott handed to him.

"Thank you, Richard." Never removing his gaze from Aurora's face, Edward kissed the garter before allowing Mr Allcott to tie it to his hat. Amid the applause that followed, he said, "Now, let us have more dancing. As we have seen, traditions must be adhered to."

The musicians played; the hour grew late. Aurora's head and feet began to ache, and she was relieved when Edward ordered one last dance before thanking and dismissing the musicians. They bowed, and while the dancers applauded, Aurora sank gratefully into a chair.

The man-servant appeared in the doorway, almost hidden behind armfuls of rosemary and branches of bay. He put his load on the floor, gave Edward an inscrutable look, and retreated.

"Oh, Eleanora, look!" exclaimed Flora. "We are going to strew the way for them!"

Aurora could not find it in her heart to look forward to the events leading up to the bride-bedding. But she made no comment while her sisters scooped up handfuls of greenery, sticking sprays in each other's hair, and trying to do the same to their mother. Mrs Eversedge resisted, though amiably. "Oh, girls, if only your father were alive to see this!"

"If Father were alive, Aurora would not be in this situation."

Everyone turned to Flora, who immediately flushed. "I mean," she continued, twisting a sprig of rosemary in her fingers, "Mr Francis – Edward, that is – would never have… Oh, do not listen to me. I have spoken hastily."

"Quite right, young lady, you have," admonished her mother. "And you must apologize."

Edward held up his hand. "My dear madam, Flora is mortified enough." An expectant silence hung upon the room as he came to Aurora's side, took her hand and drew her to her feet. "We are all aware," he declared, "that the circumstances of this wedding are not what Aurora deserves. Her father would not have parted with his daughter in anything but the traditional manner, bestowing upon her a dowry and demanding, rightly, that a contract be drawn up. But I will do everything in my power to honour and protect Aurora, and to make her as happy as she has made me today."

He leaned towards Aurora and placed a kiss upon her lips. She had never been kissed by a man before. His mouth felt soft, and the stubble on his chin scratched her skin. But Aurora did not feel the emotion a bride should feel. She felt a sense of loss. She was no longer Aurora Eversedge, eldest daughter of a Westminster mantua-maker. She was Aurora Francis, mistress of Hartford House, and whatever lay before her was in the hands of this plain, bookish, music-loving man.

A stifled exclamation came from Eleanora. She was staring at the bay leaves in her hand as if she were wondering how they had got there. "Oh, Aurora!" Advancing towards her eldest sister, she held out her arms. "I hope he loves you truly!"

And, clinging to Aurora as tightly as a child to its mother, she burst into tears.

*　*　*

The fragrance of rosemary and bay reminded Aurora of Father's garden. He had favoured flowers, but had grown herbs too, for the cooking pot and to indulge his love of orderliness. Rosemary, thyme, lavender, parsley, all in rows, and the pretty bay tree in the corner, against a sunny wall. When Aurora and her sisters were small, they were set to picking and drying the herbs for muslin bags, or to be stored in the kitchen. Aurora had loved the bursts of scent that came from the crushed thyme, the solid, shiny green of the bay leaves, the papery lavender flowers.

The smell filled the room. Edward's bedchamber was not large, but it had a pleasant aspect, with windows on two sides. Hartford House was square and well built, with a carved canopy above the door. The windowpanes sparkled, the grounds were neat, the furniture and decoration tasteful. Throughout the afternoon, Aurora's mother had not been able to hide her satisfaction at the prospect of her daughter's substantial inheritance. Later, she had demanded to make Aurora ready for bed and present her to her new husband in the bedchamber, as tradition demanded. But seeing Aurora's discomfiture, Edward had instructed Mr Allcott to take Mrs Eversedge and her younger daughters home to Dacre Street, and leave himself and his new bride in peace.

Aurora's eyes became hot as she imagined the conversation in the carriage. This stuffy, fragrance-filled room was very different from the chamber she and Flora had shared. She already missed the sight of Flora's face, animated in the candlelight, her stream of chatter mingling with the street sounds below. But Aurora had secured her freedom from that childhood existence by making her bargain with Edward. She had taken a step into a new world.

Her mother had explained what her husband would expect from her in return. She considered herself prepared, but when a knock sounded on the dressing-room door, her heart leapt. Her voice was so soft when she called for Edward to enter, she wondered if he could have heard it. She lay against the pillows, her hands folded on the counterpane, her heartbeat unsteady.

Edward opened the door. Wigless, he was wearing a nightshirt of white linen, with frilled cuffs and an embroidered hem that stopped short of a pair of white ankles and bony feet. All this Aurora had expected, but she could not help staring. She had never seen him without his wig before. The lack of it did not improve his appearance. His hair, which was very dark, was not clipped close or shaved off, like that of many men who wore wigs, but cut untidily into locks of differing lengths – short above his brow, longer behind his ears – perhaps by his own hand. Whatever his vices might be, it was clear that the personal vanity of the wealthy was not amongst them. The proportions of his head were not bad, and the neck that emerged from the ruffled collar of the nightshirt was slender, with a prominent Adam's apple.

She thought he would smile then, his face taking on the tender look she had seen at the wedding, and climb into the bed beside her. But he crossed the room to one of the windows, where he leaned on the sill, his face immobile and, to Aurora's dismay, unreadable.

"What is it, Edward?" she asked. Was he about to tell her that he was feeling too ill or exhausted to perform the act of consummation tonight? His weakness would be a constant in her married life. Consumptives never recovered. "Is there something wrong?"

He took an embroidered robe from the back of a chair and put it on. Then he came and stood beside one of the posts at the bottom of the bed, his eyes upon Aurora's face. She watched his fingers twist the fronds of the tasselled cord that secured the bed curtains.

"My dear Aurora," he began, "I am not quite as I have represented myself to you. Now I will tell you the truth, and you must decide, in the light of that truth, what you will do."

A coldness crept over Aurora, raising gooseflesh upon her arms. She sat up and pushed her loosened hair behind her shoulders. "I do not understand, sir."

He did not look at her, but worked more vigorously on the tassel. "It is quite simple. Nothing that you see around you is mine. Not this tassel, nor this curtain, nor this bed, nor this house. It all belongs to Richard, who – thank God! – has remained a loyal friend. The servants and musicians who attended to us today are associates of Richard. Actors, who have been paid for their silence. I have no carriage, no horses, no estate, no fortune." His voice quivered on the last word. He swallowed several times, composing himself. "I have nothing," he said. "Not even consumption."

Aurora said nothing. She had not the breath. She felt as if something had struck her chest with great force, squeezing the air out of it.

"My health is no more delicate than yours," continued Edward, raising his eyes to look at her at last. His voice was full of bitterness. "Though I do a mightily clever impression of a consumptive, do I not? Leaning on a stick, barely joining in the dancing, even arriving late for my own wedding? It could barely be improved. A coughing fit, perhaps? Blood on my wedding clothes? Richard warned me it was a risk, and that you might take offence at my lack of punctuality and change your mind. But I insisted. I knew you would not."

Aurora's brain buzzed with bewildered questions, interrupting one another, beginning but not ending. She could not voice any of them because her lips would not form the words. She was aware that she had pulled the covers up to her chin and was staring at her husband as if he were an exhibit at a freak show that she had paid a penny to view. Beyond that, bafflement had paralyzed her senses.

"May God forgive me," said Edward bleakly, "but I tricked you because I love you. How else would a penniless man have persuaded you to marry him?"

The bravado he had summoned in order to make this extraordinary confession had deserted him. In the candlelight the rich colours of his robe contrasted with the pallor of his face. He remained standing for a moment longer, kneading his hands. Then he untied the tasselled cords one by one and let the bed curtains fall. Taking a candle from a side table, he sat on the bed, holdng the candle so that its flame would illuminate his face, and Aurora's.

"I know you are astonished," he said, his voice both tender and urgent, "but I swear before God that what I am about to tell you is the truth."

At last, Aurora found words.

"Sir, no more!" In the small, candlelit space, their

shadows thrown weirdly upon the bed curtains, she addressed him as calmly as her thudding heart would allow. "Mr Allcott will be returned with the carriage by now. I will prevail upon him to take me home." Her throat contracted. She absolutely *would not* cry but she could not suppress her outrage. "What a good joke it must be for you and Mr Allcott, and his play-acting 'associates'! A clandestine marriage with a willing girl! Dear God, only a madman or a criminal would perpetrate a falsehood on this scale!"

"I beg you, Aurora—"

She held up her palm. "Do not speak to me. I do not know to what end you sought to humiliate me, but you will have no further opportunity to do so." She pushed aside the blankets, fought her way between the heavy curtains and put her bare feet on the floor. "I must leave this house without more ado."

Edward did not speak. His face was stony.

"We made a bargain," she reminded him angrily. "Your money for my flesh. Well, sir, no money, no flesh!"

She had no robe, but her cloak lay upon the window seat. She gathered it into her arms and went towards the dressing-room, where she had left her other clothes. The handle turned, but nothing happened. Her shoulder hit the door. There was no doubt it was locked. She flew to the bedroom door and tried its handle, equally fruitlessly.

The desire to scream for help fought with the certain knowledge that Mr Allcott had not yet returned, and the impostor servants had already gone. No one else was in the house. Aurora tried to breathe; she tried to think. She was ready to plead, or even fight, but she must escape.

Edward's black eyes glowed as he walked towards her. She yelped in fear, but he stopped before he was near enough to touch her. "You are quite correct," he said steadily, "we did make a bargain, and I am determined to keep my half of it, as I assured you. You may not give me your flesh, but I, God willing, may yet give you my money."

Aurora's breath had shortened so severely that her lungs burned. She could not control her fear. In the face of imprisonment by this man to whom she had promised herself, but who by his own admission was a liar and a deceiver, she could not find courage. "I am frightened," she gasped.

"There is no need. But I cannot allow you to leave this room until I have told you the reason for my shameful behaviour. When you have heard me, you will be free to do as you consider best."

Aurora put on her cloak, thinking busily. Another bargain had presented itself. "I will hear you, sir, if you will unlock the door."

"I cannot do that."

"Then I cannot hear you."

"You are stubborn."

"I am intelligent. You told me so yourself."

He contemplated her for a moment, neither smiling nor frowning. Calculating, perhaps. Then he drew a bunch of keys from the pocket of his robe.

Aurora stood aside while he unlocked the door. He stepped back, the keys still in his hand, his eyes still upon her. But by the time he had drawn breath to speak she had pulled the heavy door a few inches open and slipped through. Her bare feet slapping the flagstones, she ran along the gallery and down the stairs. Her heart pounded; her temples throbbed. At last, tears escaped, half blinding her as she ran. How could this have happened? How could everything she had believed be false? She desired only to get away from this place, and from Edward Francis.

She stopped at the bottom of the stairs. Where was he? Why was he not following her?

The house was utterly silent. The lighted tapers on the walls of the hallway showed that the main door was secured by bolts and an iron bar. Moonlight threw patterned shadows from the small-paned windows. The door to the dining room stood open, revealing the remains of the wedding breakfast. The actors had left the clearing-up, apparently, for Mr Allcott's real servants.

Aurora's legs were trembling. Her tears cooling on her cheeks, she sat down on the bottom stair. She was alone, at the mercy of a man who was not the fool she had taken him for. He had unlocked the door knowing perfectly well she would flee. She might escape Richard Allcott's bedchamber, but she could not escape his house. If she ventured out at this hour, dressed only in a nightdress and cloak, with no carriage or driver, and not knowing the way from Hartford House to Dacre Street, she would not get far.

For a moment she wondered wildly if she could take a horse from the stables and ride to London, relying upon strangers to set her on the road to Westminster. But she had been brought up in the city, and was no horsewoman. She leaned her head against the banister post, beset by the weariness of defeat.

"Aurora," said Edward from the top of the stairs. "You will freeze to death. Come back to the bedchamber. I swear

I will leave you alone there, once you have heard me out, which you promised to do if I opened the door."

She pulled her cloak closer around her. "I care nothing for your 'swearing', sir."

The sound of his footsteps as he descended the stairs jolted Aurora's heart once more. She could not fight down her fear of this man, who, careless of the fact that he had deceived her so wantonly, continued to press his request to be heard. She huddled at the edge of the staircase, clamping her teeth together to stop them chattering. She was cold, to be sure, and fear was making her colder. She drew her bare feet under her nightdress, waiting for his next words.

"If you will not return to the bedchamber, will you come into the dining room?" he asked, sitting down beside her on the stair. "The fire in there has not quite gone out."

Aurora's instinct was to refuse. But refusal would result, at best, in a lonely, freezing night followed tomorrow by a humiliating return to her mother's house. How she had longed to get away from there! But now it was safety, not adventure, that she craved. She must not give in to instinct; she must use the intelligence her husband insisted she possessed, and consider the alternative.

She thought quickly. Perhaps Edward had a good reason for his elaborate deception. If he was indeed a villain, and had tricked her in order to ruin her, he would surely have saved the truth for tomorrow morning. But he had not taken advantage of her innocence. He had respected her virtue. In return, it may be wise to respect his request.

Tentatively, she spoke. "Do I have your word, sir, that you will not touch me?"

"You have my word, madam."

"Then…" She could not stop trembling. She must get warm. "Then I will come with you, and hear you. But I make no promise beyond that."

Her hair, hanging untidily over her face, made a screen through which she could see his expression, but he could not so clearly see hers. His evident relief struck her so hard that she studied his face for a few moments. Was it indeed true that beside her sat a decent man driven to trickery for reasons he was desperate to explain? Or was he a better actor than the men his friend had hired?

"Thank you," he said simply. "Now, shall we sit by the fire?"

Having promised not to touch her, Edward did not offer Aurora his hand. She pushed herself up with the aid of the banister post and followed him through the open door of the dining room. Neither of them mentioned the wreckage of the banquet on the table. Aurora sat on the bench beside the fire, wrapping her feet in her cloak. She wondered if she had ever been so cold in April before.

"I am not an impostor, if that is what you dread," said Edward, bending to stoke the near-dead fire. "My father, Mr Henry Francis, was an advisor to King William, and my mother, Elizabeth, one of Queen Mary's favourite ladies-in-waiting. My mother died some years ago, but my father, as you know, is lately taken from me. He was well loved by His Majesty, and well rewarded. He left a large fortune, a London house and an estate in Lincolnshire. I am his only heir, but I am penniless."

He straightened up and sighed. Not, Aurora thought, in self-pity. It was the sigh of a wounded, defeated man.

She studied him from behind her veil of hair as he settled himself in a chair.

"I have not inherited anything," he continued. "No fortune, no property. My father altered his will and bequeathed it all to a man who was once his good friend, but became his enemy. And the document seems perfectly genuine." He leaned towards her, his fingers linked in an attitude of supplication. "But I am convinced my father's sudden disinheritance of me is a vile falsehood contrived by criminal means."

Aurora pushed back her hair. "Criminal?"

"In short, my father was murdered," said Edward. His voice became animated. "The murderer forged his signature on the altered will." His eyes, so impenetrably dark they reflected the struggling flames, searched her face. "I am determined to expose this crime, and avenge it in my father's name."

The distant call of an owl was the only sound. Fatigue rushed over Aurora. This had surely been the longest day of her life. She tensed her muscles, fearing that if she did not, sleep would overwhelm her. But Edward was still watching her, willing her to reply.

"I can scarce believe it," she confessed.

His face took on an expression of sympathy. "You are bewildered, of course, and wearied by today's events. I will be as brief as I can, but I must tell you the story." He took his gaze from her face and concentrated it upon his clasped hands. "My father, myself and a party of friends celebrated his fifty-first birthday on the seventh of December last, at Marshcote, our country house. On the eleventh of December, he returned alone to London. On the twelfth, he was found dead by the housekeeper. I rushed to our house in Mayfair as soon as I heard. It was apparent that my father had been struck down by some sudden indisposition and had died where he stood. The physician declared him dead from a convulsion, or from eating something bad. And when the will was read, to everyone's astonishment it was found that the beneficiary had been changed from myself to one Josiah Deede, a former close friend of my father's."

"But surely a will cannot be changed without a lawyer to witness it?" Aurora could not help asking, though her interruption would keep her longer from her bed.

"There *is* a lawyer's signature upon it," said Edward patiently. "That of my father's attorney, Lord Snaresborough. The will is dated the fourteenth of June last year. Lord Snaresborough died in a riding accident on the twentieth of June, less than a week later. Why he should have committed his signature to my father's extraordinary request remains a mystery. I have spoken to his widow and his associates, but none of them can throw any light on it. Needless to say, I contested the will."

"And what happened?"

"I could not convince Sir John Wilkinson, who presided at the contesting, that mischief was afoot, and the will was allowed to stand."

"Sir John Wilkinson?" Aurora was surprised. This judge was one of the few of the Catholic faith who had retained their positions in the Protestant court of King William. She could only conclude that his connections, his wealth and his will were stronger than those of his opponents.

"Josiah Deede also follows the Roman church," explained Edward. "His conversion to it was at the root of my father's estrangement from him. And he is himself an attorney, so who knows what corruption may have taken place? Lawyers, as anyone will tell you, are not always to be trusted."

"True," said Aurora ruefully. She had heard her father say the same thing. "But can you not confront this man? Surely, the fact that he worships at the same altar as Sir John Wilkinson cannot keep a murderer from the gallows?"

"It is useless to confront him!" retorted Edward. "He will deny all. My father's signature is there on the will for all the world to see. I must find proof before I accuse him, or I will find *myself* on the wrong side of the law."

Aurora had heard something in Edward's voice that had not been there before. "You will not confront this man because you *fear* him," she said. "Are you afraid that if he has murdered once, he will murder again?"

He tapped the arms of his chair, looking into the fire. Aurora saw his throat move as he swallowed repeatedly. "Yes, I fear him, and I have reason to." His intense gaze fell once more upon Aurora, but she did not flinch. "How old were you in sixteen eighty-eight?" he asked. "I was thirteen. Do you remember the tumultuous events of that year? The 'Glorious Revolution', as some call it?"

Aurora considered. "I was no more than five years old. But a couple of years later, I remember playing a game with my sisters called 'Sending the Old King Packing'. Poor Eleanora was the Old King, and we would shoo her from the room and slam the door after her. I was always the New Queen, dressed in an old petticoat of my mother's. Flora would be the New King from Holland, with a paper crown and the worst Dutch accent in Christendom."

"Thus are great events remembered in children's rhymes and games," said Edward grimly. He leaned forward and spoke with urgency. "That revolution, which sent King James into exile, may have been bloodless, Aurora, but his Catholic supporters favour another revolution, which we all fear will not be so bloodless. Josiah Deede supports King James's claim to the throne and, like many converts, he is a religious zealot. He hates Protestants with extraordinary fervour."

Aurora frowned. "Why did he convert, when those of the Catholic faith are so ill-favoured at court?"

"For the usual reason," said Edward grimly. "Fortune. Shortly after my parents married, Deede too chose a wife, a Catholic woman who brought him great riches, amassed by her family from the slave trade. My father, though repelled by his friend's conversion, was a tolerant man. He tried to continue in Deede's society. But Mrs Deede would not allow it, and Josiah Deede became irrevocably estranged from my family."

Despite Edward's best efforts to coax the fire into life, it sent out little warmth. A bone-deep chill had descended upon the room, and upon Aurora. "Intolerance is the cause of many wars, my father used to say," she observed bleakly.

Edward nodded. "That is true. But jealousy is the cause of many quarrels. You see, when our present king and queen ascended the throne, Josiah Deede was banished from court, while my father rose in King William's favour. Deede began to put about untrue gossip, saying my father was a gambler who would soon be bankrupt, and that he neglected his family. My father tried to keep this from me, but of course as I grew up I could not help but hear it.

Josiah Deede's son, who frequents coffee houses, continues to spread vile rumours, about me as well as my late father. And of course, my father's final act of disinheriting me merely adds fuel to the fire of such slander."

Edward's passionate telling of the story made such a cold-blooded plot seem more likely than Aurora ever would have imagined. Her heart trembled at the thought of the anguish the death of her mother in such circumstances would bring upon her and her sisters. "You are quite convinced of this, are you?" she asked.

"I am. And so is Richard, who has known my family for many years."

Aurora pondered. "So what do you intend to do, to right this wrong?"

"This is where *you* enter the story." Edward's eyes were fixed upon her face. "My dear Aurora, Richard and I talked endlessly of that sweet moment of revenge, but until I saw you I could not think of a way to achieve it. What I told you of my futile search for a wife is perfectly true. You are the first woman I have ever looked upon who has stirred my heart. I confessed this to Richard, and we devised a plan.

"I would pretend I still had my riches, and try to persuade you into a clandestine marriage so that no one, *especially not my father's enemies*, would know of your existence. Who better than a pretty stranger to uncover the truth by stealth?" Forgetting his promise to refrain from touching her, he gripped her hand tightly. "God will guide me in my quest to uncover this villainy. I beg you, if you will not act as my wife, will you act as my spy?"

Aurora stared at him. "Your *spy*, sir?"

"That was my word."

Aurora's knowledge of spies was meagre. She knew, of course, that the government employed men who secretly kept watch on people suspected of subversive activity. Since the spies, too, were necessarily engaged in subversive activity, she had always wondered whether spies actually spied on other spies, and no one knew exactly who anyone else was, or what they were doing. It sounded like an impossible task.

Edward's expectant gaze was fixed on her. "Do you think you can do it?"

Aurora *did* think she could do it. She was suddenly possessed by a sense of recklessness, attracted by this opportunity to pursue freedom and adventure, with the added prospect of disguise, dissembling and deceit. But she was reluctant to betray her excitement to Edward. If he could confound her, she could confound him. She pulled her hand away. "Sir, I have little doubt that I *can* do it, but the question is whether I *will*."

He looked at her warily. "*Will* you, then?"

"Perhaps. But I have a question. How do I know that what you are telling me now is true, since you have told me so many lies?"

"Richard will confirm it," he said. Releasing her, he spread his hands as if this were too obvious to say.

"But Richard could be in league with you!"

"He *is* in league with me." Anxiety was leaking away from Edward's face. He was almost smiling. "He is my loyal supporter."

"Do not twist my meaning," Aurora told him tartly. "Richard himself could be the murderer! You and he could be engaged in an infamous plot to discredit your father's former friend, get him hanged for a crime he did not commit and steal *his* fortune!"

Edward gave a brief laugh. "I suppose we could, my dear clever Mrs Francis. And if we were, I have no doubt you would find us out within five minutes." He leaned back, contemplating her proudly. "It is clear you have the attributes required for a secret existence — suspiciousness, distrust, the desire to interrogate, the need for constant confirmation. And you have the wit to think your way out of any situation. You will make a most excellent spy, do you not agree?"

She did not laugh. "I agree to nothing, sir," she said. "But if I did, what is the first thing you would have me do?"

"The first thing," he said, with apology in his eyes, "is to dupe your mother and sisters. They must not know of your true whereabouts. They must think you live here, at Hartford House, which they believe to be *my* house. But they cannot come here, and you cannot visit them in Dacre Street until all is resolved. You must write them letters full of lies, I am afraid, about my increasingly bad health and your inability to leave the house or receive them. Richard will bring you the letters they write in reply." He regarded her carefully. "Will you agree to this temporary severance from those you love?"

Aurora did not hesitate. "If I must," she replied. "And what is the second thing?"

"To invade the Deedes' privacy. Josiah Deede has a son and a daughter. My father said the son was a foppish bully, and the daughter, scarred by the smallpox, a recluse. I never saw any of the Deedes until the will-contesting, which was attended by Josiah and his son, who looked much as my father described." His gaze flicked to Aurora's face, then away again, as if embarrassed. "It is with this son, whose name is also Josiah, and his sister, whose name I do not know, that you must engineer a meeting. You are about the sister's age. You must disguise your identity, enter the Deedes' house, penetrate their daily lives, ingratiate yourself with them and search for evidence of their father's guilt."

Aurora did not speak. A foppish bully and a recluse. Enter, penetrate, ingratiate, search. She let her chin drop to her chest and rested her forehead upon her hand.

"Are you feeling unwell?" asked Edward.

"No, merely fatigued." She raised her eyes to his, which remained watchful. "If I agree to be your spy, it will be on these terms. I will do it for one month only, from this day until the same date next month. During that time you will not share my bed, nor importune me for any favours due to a husband. If your wealth is returned, you will pay me enough to bring a handsome dowry to my future husband. That is, the man I shall marry when our sham marriage is annulled."

"And if we do not succeed within a month?" His eyes were bright, but whether with hostility, or hope, Aurora could not tell.

"Likewise," she told him, "the marriage will be annulled, and I will go back to my mother as penniless as I was when I left her."

He paused, thinking. "Then you will not seek to punish me in any way?"

"I will not. Are these terms agreeable to you?"

"They are." He nodded, frowning. "So we have made yet another bargain, have we not?"

"We have, sir," said Aurora wearily. "And now, I must go to bed. Where, pray, do you intend to sleep?"

At the Sign of the Seven Stars

Covent Garden did not resemble a garden in any way. The street Edward led Aurora down was as narrow, filthy and unevenly cobbled as any other street in London. The long shadows on each side blackened the buildings, though it was only a little after four o'clock in the afternoon.

"*Floral* Street!" Aurora observed.

Edward did not reply, but hurried on.

"I cannot keep up with you," complained Aurora. "Your legs are longer than mine, and these old cobbles are torture."

Edward was scanning the shop doorways. "Here. This is the place."

The sign that swung above the door was of the Seven Stars. It was a bookseller's. Aurora might have known Edward would choose such a lodging place. While she was out of the house he could make himself comfortable, reading volume after volume from the constant supply downstairs. She could already see the scene, and imagine the fruitlessness of her objections.

"The place looks mean," she said. "Like a frowning

face. As if it were carrying a great weight upon its brow."

Edward looked at her blankly, then turned back to the door. "You say the oddest things sometimes, Aurora."

"So I have been told."

Edward rapped on the door. "Remember," he told Aurora as they waited, "I am Edward Drayton and you are my sister, Miss Aurora Drayton. I am—"

"A writer, taking lodgings in London the better to observe humankind, as you are writing a comedy of modern manners. And your loving sister is to keep house for you," recited Aurora. "I will not forget, Edward. Why do you keep testing me?"

"Forgive me. I am anxious."

The door creaked open. A female face came round it, regarding them from under a cap made for someone with a smaller head.

"Mr and Miss Drayton," said Edward. "We are expected by Mr Marshall."

The maid stood aside. Aurora found herself in a hallway barely wide enough for two people to pass, and very dark despite the candle the maid held. Without a word, the girl led the way up the stairs.

The room above the shop was Samuel Marshall's drawing room. As they entered, Aurora took in dark panelling, heavy furniture, damask curtains. Despite the building's outside appearance, it seemed the proprietor of a Covent Garden bookshop could do quite well for himself.

"Ah, the Draytons." A man of middle age rose stiffly from his chair and bowed. As Aurora completed her curtsey she examined his countenance. A self-satisfied man, to be sure, but not arrogant. His wig was short and simple, his clothes good but long worn, his lips ready with a welcoming smile. "I would accompany you to the rooms," he told them, "but I am very gouty tonight. Mary will show you."

"Thank you, sir," said Edward pleasantly. Samuel Marshall's smile broadened. Here was a gentleman lodger who might take a glass of sherry with him now and then.

They followed Mary up a flight of narrow, uneven stairs. Aurora tried to catch Edward's eye, but he would not look at her. He must surely feel, as she did, that they were stepping into uncharted territory. What would these walls see during the next month? This foray into crime detection was audacious, and they had neither expertise nor friends to call on should something go wrong. Only Richard Allcott knew where they were, and he was sworn to utter secrecy. He and Edward had already succeeded in their first deception, of Aurora herself. But tonight she entered the netherworld of the impostor, armed only with the determination to see right done.

"There's two rooms," announced Mary bluntly.

The first was small, its only furniture a bed, a table with two hard chairs, and a wooden bench long enough for about one-and-a-half people to sit. There were no curtains, and the meagre grate did not look as if it would hold much of a fire. Aurora thanked Providence that it was springtime.

Still Edward did not look at her, but he took in his surroundings quickly, then gestured to Mary to open the door to the inner room. This turned out to be even smaller, set into the eaves, and furnished only with a bed and a table, on which Mary put the candle. Aurora went to the tiny window. The glass was too dirty to see through, but she could hear horses and passers-by in the street below.

She supposed this would be her bedroom.

Longing swept over her, to be in her real bedroom at home, falling asleep to the sounds of the dying fire and Flora's regular breathing. She ignored it. "Edward, my dear," she said, "these rooms are perfect. Will you settle with Mr Marshall, while I discuss domestic concerns with … Mary, is it?"

The maid nodded. "Breakfast brought up, no other meals," she told them. "Bedlinen provided. Washin' extra."

"Of course," said Edward. "My sister will see that you are paid for your work. Now, is there a man to help bring our luggage from the Black Swan?"

"William," said Mary in her economical way. "Don't like porterin', but if you give 'im something for 'is trouble, sir…"

Edward had already left the room. "Very well!" Aurora heard him call from the stairs. "Aurora, I will be back forthwith!"

Mary and Aurora regarded each other. "Will you bring the linen?" asked Aurora. "And candles?"

The maid gave a very small curtsey. "Yes, 'm."

She seemed to be waiting. Aurora resisted. "Very well, you may go," she said, and, in a gesture of dismissal she had often seen her mother use, began to loosen her hat-strings. "I wish to rest."

Mary took the candle and stumped down the stairs, leaving Aurora in utter darkness. She removed her hat, feeling the familiar woven straw between her fingers. Her heart trotted a little. She thought about her trunk being half carried, half dragged from the inn where Richard's carriage had deposited Edward and herself an hour ago. Before they had left Hartford House, Richard had given Edward a sealed packet that Aurora suspected contained money. Edward had shaken his friend's hand, then embraced him. "Until we meet again, my dear Richard. May God bless you," he had told him earnestly.

Aurora felt for the edge of the bed and sat on it, her brain busy. In a little under a month she would be free of her promise. Meanwhile, she must live as Miss Drayton, beholden to a husband of three days, whose only bargaining power lay in a fortune he did not possess. She was not sure that she could do what he wanted, anyway. And if Miss Drayton's true identity should be quickly exposed, who would bear the consequences?

A commotion on the stairs brought her to her feet. She felt her way to the door. In the outer room Edward and a skinny boy of about sixteen were manhandling the luggage while Mary trudged about, putting a taper to the wall candles.

"Very well, that will be all!" Edward maintained the cheerful demeanour he had obviously decided should characterize Edward Drayton's dealings with servants. "A penny for your trouble, William!" He fished in his pocket and inspected the coins in his palm. "No, tuppence!"

The boy disappeared with no word of thanks, followed sulkily by Mary. Edward closed the door. "Good God, what a useless boy!" He reached into the deep pocket in the lining of his coat and produced a bottle of wine. "This will warm us, inside and out." He set the bottle on the table. "No glasses, but you are not averse to drinking from the bottle, are you? This miserable place needs something to cheer it up, and a bottle of wine is as good as anything."

Aurora would rather have had a hot cup of chocolate from a coffee house, but she smiled at Edward's expectant face. His demeanour was strikingly different from that of the man who had proposed to her in her mother's parlour. He no longer stooped; his back was as straight as her own. He wore a plain coat over a waistcoat trimmed with a narrow twirl of gold thread, and a short wig. His eyes remained shadowed, to be sure, but they had lost their blank look.

"You look as pleased with yourself as a truant schoolboy," she told him.

"I feel a little like a truant schoolboy," he confessed, pushing the stopper from the bottleneck and wiping the lip on his shirt-tail. His anxiety, which must have been relentless throughout the period since his father's death, had given way to euphoria. He sat down at the table. "Here, you have the first draught."

Aurora immediately felt the wine comforting her chilled body. She drank again, then passed the bottle to Edward, who closed his eyes in satisfaction as he swallowed. Then he put the bottle down and turned his gaze steadily upon Aurora. There it was again: the thin, unsmiling mouth, shadowed cheeks, bright black eyes. The same face that had beseeched her to take pity on him at Dacre Street that day. And yet, now she had become more familiar with it, it was not the same face. It was no longer the face of a lovelorn consumptive. Aurora could not describe it as the face of a man of action, but in it she saw conviction and purpose.

"Drink again," he said. "You are shivering."

Aurora put the bottle to her lips but took a very small

sip, unwilling to fortify her nerves at the risk of blunting her judgement. "I am shivering, I confess, because I am fearful."

"I doubt it not," Edward assured her gently. "If Josiah Deede discovers you are an impostor, I cannot predict what he will do."

"We neither of us can." She took another small sip. "I do not know what to think. This has happened so quickly; my brain is a-whirl."

He again took the bottle. "Your brain is about to be tested. You must begin your task tonight."

"Tonight?" Aurora was surprised. "What would you have me do?"

"Attend the play at the Theatre Royal."

"Alone?"

"Alone."

It was rare for a young woman to appear unchaperoned in public, even at the notoriously laissez-faire Theatre Royal in Drury Lane.

"But—" began Aurora.

"You must seem friendless, or there is no point."

"But why must I go there?"

Edward leaned towards her. "The actor who played my man-servant yesterday is acquainted with Josiah Deede's son," he explained. "He says Deede the younger is at Drury Lane almost every night. He will be one of the rowdiest of the 'bloods', you may be sure. You must draw attention to yourself in some way so that he notices you, and when he sees that you are alone, he may approach you."

"But how will I know him?"

"You will not," replied Edward tolerantly. "But

someone will. Half of fashionable London will be there. If you use that brain, a-whirl or not, you will find him."

"And if I fail?" Aurora was beginning to wish she had not taken even one mouthful of the wine.

"Then we will try again tomorrow night."

"We?"

He gave her a sheepish look. "Do not scold me, Aurora. This plan will only work if the Deedes suspect nothing. Father and son have seen me, but they have never laid eyes on you. Now, get your hat."

"My dear, are you alone? How shocking!"

"Not quite alone," Aurora replied to the hawk-nosed woman who had taken the seat next to hers. She hoped the woman was shocked only by her solitude, and not her appearance. Having no knowledge of the fashions of the Theatre Royal, and no time to find out, she had donned the dress she had been married in. Strenuous tugging on her corset-strings had produced a bosom more uplifted than usual, over which she had resisted the temptation to place a lace kerchief, and she had added a bunch of pink and blue ribbons to the brim of her new hat. With one of her hands she held a draw-string bag in a pink striped material – a cast-off of Flora's – and with the other she put up her lace-trimmed mask in front of her face. "My mask and I are good companions, madam."

"How droll you are! And how *very* pretty!" the woman exclaimed in delight. "I insist that you lower that mask immediately, and permit the gentlemen to see your beauty." Her gaze flicked around the auditorium and up to the boxes. "I see several of them have noticed you already, and are asking one another who you are. Tell me, where is your mama?"

Aurora lowered her mask and gave a small sigh. "I confess, madam, I have no mama, or papa. My elder brother and I have come but lately to London. He is in ill health, and stays at our lodging day after day. But I so long to meet people! I gather that to attend the theatre is permissible, as long as I choose a seat in a suitable part of the theatre, which I hope I have done."

"Oh, you certainly have!" The woman – whose décolletage and short, lace-flounced sleeves seemed to Aurora more appropriate to a younger woman than their wearer – shifted in her seat, indicating her neighbour, a man older than herself, with an important wig and a face as round as hers was long. "This is where all the best people sit. May I introduce my husband, Mr Horace Fellowes? I am Mrs Anne Fellowes. And you are…?"

"Miss Drayton. Aurora is my name," said Aurora, nodding a greeting. "I am very pleased to meet you both."

Mr Fellowes opened his mouth, but his wife did not allow him to speak. "Aurora! Divine name!" she cried. "We shall take care of you, my dear Miss Drayton, and introduce you to whomever you wish to meet. We know everyone, do we not, Mr Fellowes? And Miss Drayton is all alone! Her brother is in ill health, you see…"

The play was beginning, but the spectators were more interested in one another than in the performance. Aurora, who had not been to the theatre since before her father died, could not resist watching the actors for a few minutes, and admiring the opulence of their costumes. But the play was not what she had come here for. She put up her mask and observed the audience.

Aurora was the only unescorted young woman present. There were plenty of girls whose behaviour left no one in any doubt of their husband-seeking intentions, but they were in groups, or at least pairs. As for the young men, whose interest in Aurora had been pointed out by Mrs Fellowes, they crowded noisily into seats as near as possible to, or even on, the stage.

"Women whisper and giggle; only men shout and guffaw," was one of Mrs Eversedge's favourite admonishments, particularly of Flora's more exuberant behaviour. Aurora noticed plenty of all four activities, and the resultant hubbub which rose in volume whenever the audience showed its appreciation of something in the play.

She was amused when one of the actors, losing patience at the constant interruptions, invited a young man to come and play the part himself. The young man, whose seat was at the side of the stage, made to do so, but was pulled back by his companions. During the uproar, Aurora got a good view of the men Edward had referred to as the "bloods".

Bewigged, gorgeously dressed in silk waistcoats, white stockings and silver-buckled shoes, with decorated sword sheaths at their sides and plumed hats on their heads, their behaviour was as flamboyant as their appearance. They conversed continually, turning or even standing in order to address a friend several yards away. One group was playing cards, ignoring the action of the play altogether. Aurora could not help feeling a little offended on behalf of the actors. Why did these wealthy young men not go to a coffee house, where they could be as noisy and objectionable as they liked with no trouble to anyone but themselves?

Edward had said that if Josiah Deede's foppish son was anywhere in the theatre tonight, he would be amongst the bloods. He was probably one of the best dressed, having adorned himself using Edward's money. If he were here tonight, she must make his acquaintance at all costs. But, she wondered, how could she possibly find out which one he might be?

"Did you enjoy the play, my dear?" asked Mrs Fellowes as the actors took their bow.

"Very much," replied Aurora. "Especially the impromptu entertainment provided by our friend over there." She nodded towards the unfolding comic scene as the young man who had tried to take the stage was hastened to the door, so drunk he was scarcely able to stand, but still protesting that he was as good an actor as anyone. "And it was quite free of charge!"

Mrs Fellowes laughed. "Oh, I have seen that fellow do worse than that. Once he tried to carry off the leading lady over his shoulder. He is always intoxicated, I am afraid to say. I do not know why the management of this theatre does not ban him."

"Because he is rich, perhaps? And has many friends?"

"Aye, very likely," smiled Mrs Fellowes.

Aurora seized her opportunity. "Do you know his name? Is he a titled gentleman?"

Mrs Fellowes tapped Aurora lightly on the arm with her fan. "You may be lately arrived in London, but I see you are quickly finding your way in society!"

Aurora smiled archly.

"He is indeed a titled gentleman," continued Mrs

Fellowes. "The younger son of the Earl of Strathnairn. Neither his father nor his elder brother can do anything to persuade him to be more serious. Or more sober, if you will forgive my little play on words."

Aurora giggled obediently. "They evidently have a task on their hands! And do you know any of the young men who accompanied him tonight? If there is a 'sober' one amongst them I would dearly love to know his name!"

"Now, let me see…" Mrs Fellowes frowned and pursed her lips. "I saw Lord Meethorpe, and that awful man Henry Mathias who leers at all the women, married or not. He has even made eyes at *me*, my dear, if you can believe it!"

Aurora bowed her head politely. "And who else?" she prompted. They had left their seats and were being carried, it seemed to Aurora, upon the lava-flow of the departing audience. She had seldom felt so hot and in need of fresh air.

"Oh, Mr Thomas Field was there as usual. He is some sort of writer, I believe, though like all of them he never seems to do any work. My husband, who knows his father well, says the family despairs of him."

Aurora was beginning to despair too. Mrs Fellowes had said that she and her husband knew everyone, and would introduce Aurora to whomever she liked. But here they were, surrounded by people, and she had not met anyone. She decided to clutch at a straw. "May I be introduced to Mr Thomas Field, if we can locate him?" she asked. "Since Mr Fellowes knows the family. My brother is a writer, you see, and writers always like to make one another's acquaintance."

"You are so right, my dear!" The crowd was thinning

out. Mrs Fellowes stood on her toes and scanned the remaining faces. "Oh! That might be him, with the brown hat. No, it is not." She turned to Aurora, dismayed. "I fear we are too late, and he and his friends are already in some inn, carousing, I dare say."

"Alas, but no matter," said Aurora. "I shall come to the theatre again soon."

"Then you must come with *us*," said Mrs Fellowes kindly. "Mr Fellowes, tell Miss Drayton where she will find our house. You are welcome to call, my dear. I am always at home in the afternoons."

By this time they had reached the steps in front of the theatre. Flares lit the bluish May night. Despite the lateness of the hour, Covent Garden was still noisy with carriages, horses and the hum of conversation. Aurora could smell the familiar stench of the wagons carrying the contents of each dwelling's "house of office". Aurora had no use for this polite term. At home they always called it the privy.

"You will find us in Tavistock Street," Mr Fellowes informed her. "The house next to the shop at the sign of the Sun and Falcon."

"Thank you, sir."

Although her companions had not yet departed, Aurora felt very lonely. This evening's escapade had not proved entirely fruitless, but she wished she had something more newsworthy than her meeting with this friendly couple to report to Edward. At least she could assure him that he had been right to choose a young girl as his accomplice. How quickly her lack of companions, female or male, had been noticed!

"Why, Celia, my dear!" came Mrs Fellowes's excited

voice. "Have you been here all evening? How ever did I miss you?"

Aurora turned to see her new acquaintance enthusiastically embracing a fair-haired girl. This girl, who was shorter of stature than Aurora, was finely dressed in a beribboned yellow gown and embroidered underskirt, and gazed upon the world from blue eyes in a heart-shaped face.

"Yes, we were here," she said, smiling. "I saw you from the balcony, Mrs Fellowes, but you were so busy speaking to your companion I did not call to you."

The thought flitted across Aurora's mind that Mrs Fellowes's company, useful though it was to Aurora herself, might not be so desirable to other young people. But this girl maintained her countenance and regarded Aurora with a very engaging air.

"Is this young lady a relative of yours, Mrs Fellowes?" she asked. "I do not believe we have been introduced."

"No, we are not related, more's the pity, considering her beauty." Mrs Fellowes grinned at both girls, who smiled obligingly in return. "This is Miss Aurora Drayton, who is recently moved to London and is tonight making her first appearance at the theatre."

Aurora curtseyed self-consciously, aware that her dress was not so near the height of fashion as that of the golden-haired girl, nor her hairstyle so intricate, nor her hat so gorgeously trimmed. But the torture of the tight corset had been worth it; the boldness of her décolletage and the smallness of her waist could stand up to any scrutiny.

"Aurora," said Mrs Fellowes, "this is Miss Celia Deede, the daughter of my late good friend Mrs Philomena Deede. Celia and her family live in Tavistock Street too."

Aurora's heart had leapt so suddenly that she almost missed Celia Deede's next, gently spoken words.

"I must correct you there, my dear Mrs Fellowes. We have not been your neighbours for several weeks. We live in Mill Street now."

"Of course you do! I had quite forgotten. And do you like your new house?"

"Very much, thank you," said Celia sweetly. "Oh! Here is Joe."

A gentleman approached. Aurora needed only one glance to absorb his well-kept coat decorated with wide bands of gold at the cuffs, his polished boots, his unostentatious wig and white-plumed hat, tall stature, confident bearing and fair face. He was certainly the most handsome man she had seen tonight.

"This is my brother Josiah," said Celia to Aurora. "He is always called Joe, as Josiah is also my father's name. Joe, this is Miss Drayton."

Joe Deede looked at Aurora with undisguised admiration. So undisguised that Mrs Fellowes lost no time in acting upon it.

"Miss Drayton is without an escort, Joe, if you can believe it. Her brother is in ill health and does not leave the house, but she craves company. And who can blame her? Such a pretty thing!"

Joe Deede bowed. "Miss Drayton, if you will allow me, may I offer to convey you home in our carriage?"

"I thank you, sir," said Aurora, "but I have no need of a carriage. I live very near."

"But you cannot walk alone through dark streets!" protested Celia. "Please allow us to accompany you."

"Thank you," said Aurora again, "but there is no need. I insist."

Celia Deede gave her a curious look, though not, Aurora thought, an offended one. "Very well." Her gaze touched her brother, then came back to Aurora. "As you please. But will you call on us in Mill Street? Come tomorrow, for dinner at two o'clock, and meet my father. Since you are newly arrived in the city you must be in need of friends, and we have hundreds! It is the house on the corner of Conduit Street and Mill Street in Mayfair. There is a stone horse-trough outside, with an inscription to St Christopher."

Aurora curtseyed. Her mouth had dried so much that she could not immediately utter her thanks. This opportunity to ingratiate herself with the Deedes had occurred so swiftly she could hardly muster her thoughts. Celia Deede had taken a fancy to her and, for her part, she warmed to the girl's smiling, audacious, but courteous, manners. To make further acquaintance with this smooth-complexioned girl and her utterly un-foppish brother was vital, though she must do it without revealing anything of her true self. "Thank you, Miss Deede," she said. "You are very kind."

Celia Deede dropped a small curtsey, her eyes on Aurora's face. "The pleasure, Miss Drayton, is all mine."

Edward must have heard Aurora's footfalls on the stairs. Wigless, in his nightshirt and house robe, with a candle in his hand, he was waiting for her at the open door.

Aurora walked in, removed her gloves, untied her hat-strings and faced him. "I met them."

Edward closed the door. "Father and son?" he asked, bright-eyed.

"No, son and daughter. Celia Deede is not scarred. Neither is she a recluse. Indeed, she told me she has hundreds of friends. "

Edward's mouth opened, but he did not speak.

"Celia is a delightful name, is it not?" observed Aurora. "As delightful as her countenance and clothes, both of which are of the greatest beauty. Her brother is handsome too, as you no doubt know, and they are both very well-mannered. They insisted I did not go home alone."

His eyebrows rose and his jaw fell. "You did not allow them to escort you here?" he exclaimed, horrified. "Of all the—"

"Of all the imbecilic things to do? Good God, Edward, how little you think of me!"

Exhausted, she sat down at the table. She removed her hat and rested her forehead upon her fingertips, rubbing her temples in the hope of relief from an insistent headache. "Of course I did not lead them to this place! I insisted I be permitted to return home alone. What Joe and his sister made of my obstinacy I do not know, but they showed me nothing but kindness."

Edward sat down on the edge of his bed and stared at the dirty floor. *"Joe?"*

Aurora's shoulders drooped. Her body felt numbed by the enormity of the subterfuge she had embarked upon at the expense of such amiable people. How bewildered they must be at her refusal of their protection!

"Very well, you did not give them your address," said Edward, looking up. "But did they give you theirs?"

"They told me they live in Mill Street, off Conduit Street, in Mayfair. At the house by the stone horse-trough."

Aurora watched Edward absorb this news. The Deedes had recently moved, of course, to the address which was rightfully his own. But his voice and countenance remained steady. "How long will you wait before you call?" he asked.

"I am to go tomorrow, to dine with them and their father."

"And if they wish to return the call?"

"I will explain that my brother is in poor health and we do not receive visitors."

The candlelight licked Edward's face. His lips were compressed into a line. Neither he nor Aurora spoke for a long time. At last, she could bear it no more. "Edward, I confess myself baffled," she said. "How could your father have hated these people so much? They are pleasant, I assure you. And they have many friends. I cannot understand how you have not met them before. You must have been kept apart by the unceasing vigilance of your families."

Edward did not look at her. Aurora mustered her courage and softened her tone. "Is it possible your suspicions are unfounded?"

He rose, went to the empty fireplace and set the candle on the mantel. "No, it is not possible."

"Why not?"

"Aurora, have pity!" These words were expelled with such force that they almost killed the candle flame. "Somewhere in that house is the answer to the questions I have been asking myself since the day my father died. How did he die, and why did he disinherit me? I must know the truth, and you have agreed to help me discover it. Are you so taken in by the Deedes' appearance of amiability – the very *amiability* that makes no one suspect them – that you will abandon our cause?"

He rubbed his face wearily. Though it was a sentence of his own making, this evening's incarceration in the attic rooms, waiting for news, had taken its toll on his spirits. Aurora could see how unsettled he was. She rose and went to him, chastened. "Of course not," she said gently. "And you know, Edward, the plan is working. *Your* plan. The Deedes are pleased to welcome a friendless female into their circle, exactly as you said they would be. I do not believe they see me as a threat."

He considered her words, a muscle in his cheek working. "No, they see you as a potential companion for the girl and a match for her brother. It cannot be by chance that you met them. They must have been watching you all evening. Deede no doubt has an eye for a beautiful maid. It must be very flattering, having *two* men at your feet."

"Oh, Edward, what nonsense! I have no dowry and no family connections!"

"That did not stop *me*, either from loving you or marrying you."

"But you had other reasons for your courtship of me," retorted Aurora.

His face no longer showed the inscrutability she had so often tried to fathom. There was misery in his eyes and tension in the set of his chin. "Do you doubt that I love you?"

Aurora sighed. "Joe Deede will never ask a Protestant woman to marry him, as well you know."

"It is not a proposal of marriage the man has in mind!" cried Edward scornfully. "It is a … a flirtation. A gratification of his desires."

Aurora tried to remain calm. "Edward, hear me. You wished me to ingratiate myself with Josiah Deede's son, but are jealous when I do. So—"

"That was when I thought he was a fop and a fool! But now you say he is neither of those things!"

"So what would you have me do?" demanded Aurora. "Do you seriously imagine that I – who would not consent to the 'gratification of the desires' of a man who married me under false pretences – will now succumb without scruple to the attentions of the first handsome man I see?"

He had the grace to hang his head. "Aurora…"

"And if Joe Deede *should* wish to court me," she continued frostily, "he had better begin forthwith. He has less than a month, remember."

They regarded each other for a moment. Neither of them pointed out that Edward's own courtship of Aurora had lasted less than a quarter of an hour.

"I beg you, forgive me," said Edward wearily. "I have not the right to be jealous. Though jealousy was never a respecter of rights."

Aurora was strongly tempted to sulk. But she resisted; this was no time for pettiness and flouncing. "Have no fear," she told him. "When I go to Mill Street tomorrow, I shall be wary of everything, including Joe Deede's attentions. I will encourage them, because I am trying to *ingratiate* myself with the family. But that does not mean I am being disloyal, to my husband or my God. It is a *pretence*."

He nodded. "Of course. I understand that, and I must tolerate it as best I can."

"Very well." Aurora was suspicious of this apparent humility. His eyes were still watchful. "Edward," she ventured, "have I displeased you?"

"Not at all." He shook his head. "Your night's work has

been very successful. But I am disturbed by the discovery of my father's lies. He taught me always to be truthful."

Aurora almost laughed aloud. Truthful!

"Then…" she began in an ironic tone, "would he not be sorely grieved by the deceptions you perpetrated upon me, and are continuing to perpetrate upon the Deedes, on his behalf?"

His black eyes flicked to hers. He had heard the irony. "Yes, he would. But think of the alternative! Everyone in society whispering about my sudden disinheritance? Years of bearing my disgrace without prospect of redress? I cannot imagine it."

Pity and impatience fought each other for a moment in Aurora's heart. But the bleakness of Edward's countenance decided the matter. "Then I make you a promise," she said stoutly. "Tomorrow, I will find a way to bring Henry Francis into the conversation. If I detect the smallest chink in the Deedes' facade I will not rest until I have something to report to you."

Edward took hold of her hand, massaging absent-mindedly the finger where her wedding ring, which she had removed within twenty-four hours of her marriage, should be. "I know you will not," he said with wistful satisfaction.

Despite the firmness of her words, a sudden stab of apprehension caught Aurora unawares. What would she face tomorrow? She withdrew her hand, retrieved her hat and gloves from the table and opened the door to the inner room. "And now," she said, "I confess myself exhausted. I bid you goodnight."

Edward's Library

Aurora did not know the streets of Mayfair, though she knew the area was a good address. Many premises advertised themselves as milliners, glovers or wig shops. Others sold more unnecessary things like silver and porcelain, silk-covered cushions and gilded mirrors. She noticed the pristine books in the booksellers' window, quite different from the cracked covers and grimy pages of those offered by Samuel Marshall at the sign of the Seven Stars. Prices, no doubt, were high.

Mill Street was narrower and darker than Conduit Street, but the stone horse-trough was plain to see, with its inscription invoking St Christopher. There, on the corner, stood Edward's house.

He had been born here. His mother and father had both died here. It was here that he had learned his letters from a tutor and the violin from his beloved music master. "As a boy, I was never happier than when I was reading a book or playing my fiddle," he had told Aurora. "By the time I was eighteen I had read all my father's books, so together we embarked upon expanding his library."

They had chosen, bought, placed and stood back to admire each volume. But the years' spent building this precious library had been in vain. Like everything else in the house, it had been lost to Josiah Deede.

The house was substantial. There was no shop at the level of the street. Aurora counted three storeys, then stood back from the overhang and noticed a fourth built into the roof. All had the elegant sash windows of the wealthy. She could not quash the thought that by insisting to Edward that their marriage be annulled whatever the outcome of their quest, she had rejected the chance to become mistress of this house. And, furthermore, of Marshcote, Edward's family seat in Lincolnshire, the aspect, situation and proportions of which she could only imagine.

A man-servant answered her knock.

"Good afternoon," she said. "My name is Miss Drayton. I am expected by Miss Deede."

He opened the door for her to pass through. "Miss Deede will be down in a few minutes," he said, leading her towards the rear of the house. "Will you wait in here, if you please, Miss?"

Aurora found herself in a room which was clearly the library, though it perhaps also served as a study, and may have been a schoolroom in the past. There were many bookshelves, and a sturdy old-fashioned globe in the corner. In the centre of the carpet was a large table covered with books and papers. The space between the windows was occupied by a new, expensive cabinet, the type in which the front lowered to reveal a writing surface and many small drawers, cupboards and compartments.

Aurora suspected this writing desk was locked, but she

scrutinized it closely. There was a keyhole in the hinged front, and another in each of the three drawers below. The keyholes were all of the same type, and probably opened with the same key, perhaps similar to the key that unlocked the box in which Aurora's mother kept a yellowing bundle of Father's love letters.

The desk seemed a suitable place to begin to search for something – a private paper, an account, a legal document, anything that might incriminate Josiah Deede. She could do nothing now, but she resolved to return as soon as an opportunity arose, and conduct herself like a real spy. She must either find the key or conquer the lock by some even less legitimate means.

Above the fireplace was a painting of a country house. Aurora leaned closer to read the inscription on the frame. "Marshcote, 1656." The house was low, made of red brick, not at all imposing. Set round a courtyard, it had casement windows and many chimneys, in the style of buildings of more than a hundred years ago. It must have been in the Francis family for generations. She thought about this for a moment. Her husband's family. *Her* family, for the present. And now it had passed to the Deedes.

Celia Deede flung open the door. Dressed in a pink and green silk house robe, its flounced sleeves trailing from her wrists, and with ribbons threaded through her blonde hair, her smiling countenance was as open as that of a child.

"Miss Drayton!" she cried, taking Aurora's hands, "how lovely you look!"

Aurora had dressed in one of her two second-best gowns, a small-patterned brocade left unpaid-for by one of Mrs Eversedge's customers, and eventually, after much unhappy correspondence, bequeathed to Aurora. It was a little heavy for a spring day, and Aurora hoped her attempt to lighten it by wearing pale-coloured shoes and a modestly trimmed hat had succeeded.

"Thank you." She found herself drawn into the hall, where the man-servant waited at the foot of the stairs. "Please call me Aurora."

"And you must call me Celia," said her hostess, thrusting Aurora's cloak into the man-servant's arms. "Harrison, find Mr Joe."

Upstairs, they entered a large salon decorated in a tasteful, though not highly fashionable, style. "Joe will be here in a minute," said Celia happily. "I was at the window and saw you looking at the house from the street, but Father says I must always leave Harrison to open the door because I am the mistress of the household. You seemed very interested in our house! Do you approve?"

"Oh, yes!" Aurora gazed round the room. She saw a Turkish carpet, upholstered furniture, large portraits tastefully arranged upon pale walls, a carved fireplace, a pile of books upon a small table, work abandoned on a chair. Light streamed through tall windows, one of which was open to the spring air and the sounds of the city. The room gave off an atmosphere of calm content, as if pleasant people conversed here, and pleasant things happened.

"My father wishes to change this room," said Celia, also looking around. "He says it has too much of a woman's hand upon it. I believe it was furnished by the wife of the previous owner."

"You have not lived here long, I understand?" ventured Aurora. She sat down on the chair Celia indicated, adjusting the fall of her skirt. Her stomach seemed to be trying to escape from the top of her bodice. She tried to breathe steadily.

Celia pushed aside her crumpled work and sat down to consider Aurora's question. "Father was left this house in a will," she said, "and it is grander than where we lived before, in Tavistock Street. Joe is so pleased to be living at such a smart address!"

"You are fond of your brother," observed Aurora with a smile.

"Very fond."

"As I am of mine."

"Do tell me about your brother!" demanded Celia. "He is in ill health, is that correct?"

Aurora sighed. "I am afraid so."

"And he will not receive visitors or go out?"

"Cannot, rather than will not. He is in a consumption. Not quite at the end, but he is very ill."

"And you nurse him? How noble!"

"We have servants," said Aurora, thinking ruefully of taciturn Mary and workshy William. "And he keeps himself occupied. He is a writer."

Celia frowned. "A playwright, you mean? Or is he a – you know – a political man?"

"He is neither. He writes for his own pleasure," said Aurora gently. "And I think, under the circumstances, we can none of us begrudge him the indulgence."

"Quite so." There was a short, uncomfortable silence. Then Celia took one of the books from the table and slid Aurora a sheepish look. "Joe gave me these to read. Father says I must read, or I will be empty-headed, and he does not approve of empty-headed girls. But I confess I do not very much like reading."

Aurora smiled indulgently. "Neither do I. And like you, I have a brother who is very attentive to my education, I'm sorry to say."

She had in fact recently been working her way through the plays of Shakespeare with great enjoyment, and was looking forward to resuming her study whenever she could. But Miss Aurora Drayton's apparent ignorance of the world must be made to work in her favour as an impostor. Frowning, she inspected the titles Joe had selected for his sister. A book of sermons, a history of China, a compendium of moral tales translated from German and a small volume of household hints.

She was about to make a light-hearted comment on the choice, when she realized that the books she was handling were probably Edward's. He or his father might have sought them out and placed them upon the chosen shelf in the library, the very room where she had waited downstairs.

She dropped the book she had been scrutinizing. It was the German tales, a thick volume that fell with a thud upon the wooden floor. Hastening to retrieve it, apologizing to Celia for her carelessness and trying to hide the flush that covered her cheeks, Aurora was unprepared for what she saw when she straightened up, the book in her hand.

Joe stood before the fire, his left hand on the hilt of his sword. His weight was over his right foot; the other rested upon the empty fire basket. He was smiling tolerantly, amused by her confusion. His unadorned coat and short wig told her he was on his way to some masculine business.

She spoke as lightly as she could. "Good afternoon to

you. As you see, I am wrestling with this book, though I have not yet even opened it!"

Last night the flares outside the theatre had illuminated Joe Deede's fair looks, but had deepened the shadows cast by his hat and the side-pieces of his wig. Today he was hatless, and in the daylight Aurora saw how fresh his face truly was. Like his sister, he smiled easily, and had the same blue eyes and freckles of the fair-skinned.

"Miss Drayton," he said with studied courtesy, "how very delightful it is to see you again. I trust you are well?"

"Quite well, I thank you, Mr Deede."

"Oh, call him Joe!" interjected Celia.

Her brother bowed his acquiescence, his complexion turning pink. Perhaps Edward was right, and last night's meeting had not been by chance. Perhaps Joe Deede *had* been watching her all evening, and had sent his sister to cross the path of Mr and Mrs Fellowes and their young companion as they left the theatre. It was certainly flattering to imagine so.

"Then you must call me Aurora," she replied.

He bowed again. His blush had subsided, but his embarrassment still showed in his inability to return her gaze. His sister, seeing all, rescued him. "I trust you had a pleasant walk from Covent Garden, Aurora?" she asked conversationally.

"I did, thank you. It is a fine afternoon. And I only had to ask the way once."

"Oh!" cried Celia. "You are unfamiliar with London, are you not? If you had told us where you live, Joe would have collected you."

Joe had recovered enough to look at Aurora. "It would have been an honour."

"And yet I could not allow it, sir – I mean, Joe. My brother wishes to remain … not exactly in hiding, but…" She smoothed her skirt, feigning unease. "It is a long story. Perhaps after he has passed away…"

Joe and Celia were both looking at her questioningly. Aurora knew she would have to explain, as plausibly as she could, without slighting their hospitality.

"It is shameful," she said, inventing as she spoke, "but my brother has creditors who have become impatient. He has instructed me to make sure that no one knows where our lodging place is exactly."

"Is that why you have taken lodgings in such a…" began Celia.

"It is easy to lose oneself in Covent Garden!" supplied Joe quickly. "But we are not your brother's creditors, Aurora. It would not matter if we knew where you live."

She gave him a beseeching look. "Please, I must keep my promise to my brother. People in London know other people. They meet, they talk… He trusts no one. So no one, even you, must find us. I beg you, give me liberty to go to and fro alone."

"I do not like it," said Joe after a moment's pause, during which the expression in his eyes grew warmer, "but I will agree to it. Not for his sake, but for yours."

"Thank you, sir," said Aurora.

Joe looked at her a moment longer, then turned and slapped the mantelshelf. "Dammit, I could pay his creditors three times over!"

"But he will not allow you to, sir," insisted Aurora.

Celia pressed her hand. Her expression was so concerned that Aurora was ashamed. As Joe settled himself in a chair, she was glad to change the subject. "Are you not going out, sir?" she asked him.

"No, I am only too happy to be in the present company."

"But your appearance seems to indicate otherwise."

"Joe does not wear a house robe," explained Celia.

"Indeed I do not," he declared. "Why a man should not wear his coat and sword in his own house is beyond me. If I am to meet a lady I dress appropriately."

"Oh, Joe, do not be so serious!" cried Celia. "A house robe is a perfectly practical way of being comfortable in one's own house."

"I am comfortable enough," said her brother, as seriously as before, "in plain clothes such as these, and with a serviceable sword at my side."

Celia made a face. "My brother is very proud of his swordsmanship, Aurora, and loses no opportunity to exhibit it."

"I make no apology for my desire to wield a blade well," said Joe confidently. "It is the mark of a true gentleman."

"As are horsemanship and the ability to call a hawk," added Celia. "Joe likes nothing better than country pursuits. Do you ride, Aurora?"

"No, I confess I do not."

During the pause that followed Aurora marshalled her thoughts. She had not come here to make small talk with Joe Deede and his sister. She must not lose sight of the true reason for her visit, nor of her obligation to her husband. "May I enquire, is your father from home?" she asked.

"Yes," replied Joe. "He goes out to business, but he will be back for two o'clock dinner."

"And what is his business?" asked Aurora.

An almost unnoticeable glance passed between Joe and his sister before he answered. "He is an attorney at law. He deals in the transfer of property."

"I see." Aurora was aware of something unsaid, hovering in the air. "Well, whatever Mr Deede's business may be, he is clearly a man of means," she said, making sure her tone was that of a lightly cast remark.

Neither Celia nor Joe spoke. Aurora knew their father had two other sources of income apart from that of an attorney. One was the legitimate proceeds of his marriage to an heiress, the other the more dubious inheritance of Henry Francis's estate. But his children were hardly likely to share this information with a stranger.

Aurora glanced at the clock. It said five minutes to two. "Anyway, I anticipate with great pleasure the honour of meeting Mr Deede," she said, equally lightly. "A man with two such handsome offspring must be extremely well favoured himself."

"Flattery!" trilled Celia, smiling again. "I believe we take after our mother in *looks*, though I cannot vouch for how much of our father's *character* we have inherited. It is impossible to judge oneself."

"It is indeed," said Joe. "But all too easy to judge others."

Another silence threatened, but was averted by the sound of footsteps on the stairs and a shouted command to a servant, followed by the opening of the door.

Josiah Deede had neither the stature nor the fair complexion of his son. He was of no more than middle height, and carried the undefined waistline of the middle-aged and well fed. His clothes and hat were more decorative than Joe's, and he wore sashes across his chest and a long wig. His dark brown eyes were set deeply beneath heavy brows. Although he had something of the look of his son around his mouth, well favoured he was not.

"So this must be the famous Miss Drayton!" he exclaimed, bowing. His voice was friendly enough, but blustery and confident. He had the air of a man used to telling others what to do. "Pleasure to make your acquaintance, madam."

Aurora extended her hand. "The famous Miss Drayton?" she repeated, smiling. "Why, you had surely never heard my name until yesterday!"

Josiah Deede shook her hand energetically. "That is true, but my daughter has not stopped speaking of you since. Miss Drayton this, and Miss Drayton that. And my son" – with a meaningful look at Joe – "does not lag far behind her in singing your praises."

Joe braved his embarrassment. "And do you not now understand my enthusiasm?" he enquired of his father.

"Aye," said Mr Deede in a softer tone, gazing at Aurora's face. Then he addressed his daughter at his accustomed volume. "Is dinner ready? I am as hungry as a lion."

"And you make as much noise as one!" scolded Celia, opening the door to call the servant.

Joe was smiling at Aurora. "Come," he said, offering her his arm. "We must not have you stumble on the stairs."

The dining room was as well appointed as the salon, with two large windows, elegantly draped with dark-patterned curtains, and a polished floor. The only decoration Aurora was certain had not been placed there by the late Mrs Elizabeth Francis was a large wall-mounted crucifix, the blood drops from Christ's wounds painted a lurid red. Beside it, the candle-holders contained new beeswax candles, ready to be lit when the light faded.

As Aurora took the place indicated by Celia, between her and her father, opposite Joe, she pictured her mother's careful hoarding of beeswax, melting and making, melting and making, using every last drip so that there would be sweet-smelling candles to burn when customers came. Otherwise, she and her daughters made do with the foul odour and eye-smarting smoke of tallow candles. Aurora wondered if Joe and Celia Deede even knew the difference.

After Josiah Deede had spoken grace, he spooned soup and forked roast pork into his mouth with speed and enjoyment, tearing and offering bread, mopping up gravy, concentrating more on the food than on his guest. But when the plates were empty and the servant was pouring more wine, he turned to Aurora.

"My daughter tells me you went alone to the Theatre Royal last night, Miss Drayton. Is that correct?"

"Oh, Father!" protested Celia. "She is not *your* daughter, you know!"

Mr Deede held up his hand. "Peace! I merely wish to ask Miss Drayton if she enjoyed the play. A young lady who braves that rabble without an escort must have, in my opinion, a strong reason for it."

"I did enjoy it, very much indeed," said Aurora, "though I confess that I was led to the Theatre Royal less by its reputation for fine drama than as a meeting place. I have little opportunity for entering society, but I *must* be amongst people. It is my nature."

Josiah Deede looked sympathetic. "My dear girl,

your situation, and that of your unfortunate brother, is to be pitied indeed. But now that you have made our acquaintance, there is no reason for you to be at all lonely. You must regard our house as your own."

Aurora bowed her head. "You are very kind, sir, to provide me with such excellent hospitality. And as for the attentions of your son and daughter…"

"But we *want* to pay you attention!" said Celia eagerly. "After the play, Joe said to me, 'Look at that girl with Mrs Fellowes. I wonder who she is?' I wondered too, as I did not think Mrs Fellowes had any nieces, or at least any pretty ones. So we got in your way as you left the theatre, and sure enough, you were all alone, and in need of befriending. And I am so glad we *did* befriend you, and so is Joe, are you not, Joe?"

"Guilty as charged," said Joe, smiling, with his hand over his heart.

Celia clapped her hands in approval. Even Eleanora did this only when she forgot herself. Aurora's youngest sister considered such behaviour too childish for a thirteen-year-old, and Celia Deede was at least five years older. It was clear that as the baby of the household, Celia had been indulged since her mother's death by a doting father and brother.

"You see, Aurora?" She pushed back her chair. "Now, if you have eaten sufficient, come upstairs and drink some tea with me. Father will want to smoke a pipe" – a look of mock disapproval – "and he likes Joe to join him in a glass of Madeira after dinner. We have half an hour in which to speak of *interesting* things."

"Very well," said Aurora, rising from the table. The

gentlemen rose too, and she regarded them apologetically. "If you will excuse us, I confess I like nothing better than *interesting* things."

"Then you are made in my own image!" trilled Celia joyfully. "Except that you are prettier, of course."

Aurora knew she was not. "You are modest, Celia, and it becomes you."

"So are you, Miss Drayton," said Josiah Deede unexpectedly. "And modesty in a woman is the more becoming, the more beauty she possesses."

Aurora accepted the compliment with a dip of her head. But as she turned from the table her glance caught Joe's. His eyes were bright with approval.

Celia chattered all the way up the stairs, but Aurora was not listening. She knew that what was meant by *interesting* conversation was gossip about courtship, marriage, infidelity and illegitimacy. How could she make such things into something worth reporting to Edward?

"That will be all, Missy," said Celia to the maidservant who brought the tea tray. When the girl had gone Celia sat down on a footstool. Drawing it near to Aurora's chair, she leaned forward and kept her voice low. "May I ask, my dear Aurora, if you have any suitors?"

Aurora had not expected this. But she responded in kind, leaning towards Celia and speaking softly. "No, none at all. Have you?"

Perched on the footstool, hugging her knees, Celia turned her translucent blue eyes upon Aurora. Her face had taken on the earnestness of a child about to betray a secret. "No, but we are not discussing *me*. Aurora, you surely cannot have failed to notice my brother's attraction to you?"

Aurora obliged with an arch look, though her brain raced with unlooked-for pictures of Joe's blush when Celia insisted on the use of his first name, and his admiring glance as Aurora had left the dinner table. "He may be attracted to me if he so chooses," she said. "I have no objection. But I have not noticed any particular attentions, I must say."

"You are dissembling, Aurora! Confess it, when you look at him you are already measuring your wedding gown!" Celia hugged her knees tighter, squirming with delight. "We shall be sisters!"

Aurora failed to muster another arch look. "Celia, your imagination runs away with you. "I am sure Joe will choose a wife in good time, from those of the faith to which your family adheres."

"Oh!" Celia released her knees and stared in dismay. "You and your brother do not follow the Roman Church! I was sure you did! You see, Mrs Fellowes is from a Catholic family. She knew my mother."

Aurora managed to smile. Edward had coached her in exactly what to say when this subject presented itself. "I do not know Mrs Fellowes well. I only met her for the first time last night, and she asked me no questions about my religion." She reached for Celia's hand, hoping that the lie she was about to utter might sound more plausible if accompanied by physical reassurance. "But my late parents, though of the Protestant faith, brought my brother and me up to be tolerant of everybody's beliefs. You need have no fear."

"Then you do not think Catholics…" Celia searched for appropriate words. "You do not consider us … in the way many people do these days?" She could not voice the words "as plotters against the king", but her blue eyes searched Aurora's face, willing her answer to be the one she sought.

Aurora tried not to think of the punishment God must be storing up for her. She resolved to enter a church on her way home and ask His forgiveness. "I believe," she told Celia, "that Catholics are, for the most part, decent people like you and your family."

"So if a Catholic man were to woo you," suggested Celia with a sly look, "might you be prepared to *convert*?"

Aurora looked at the floor, hoping Celia would interpret her unease as maidenly modesty. "King James himself is a convert," she said, "and he had a great deal more to risk by his conversion than I could ever have."

Celia seemed satisfied with this. "That is true. But you know, my father is also a convert," she said moodily, "and he hates Protestants with a most un-Christian fervour, as did my mother, though I confess I do not."

"I thank you for that, Celia," said Aurora. She wished to change the subject, but could think of nothing that would bring the conversation any nearer Henry Francis, his son or the Deedes' unexpected inheritance. Into her mind came a picture of the room downstairs, with its paper-strewn table and locked cabinet. And suddenly she had an inspiration. "May I look at your library?" she asked brightly.

Celia's face went blank. "But you said you do not care for books."

"That is true, I do not. But my brother does. He likes nothing better than to read, when he is not employed in writing, but his collection of books is small. Would you mind if I were to borrow one or two of yours for him?"

"I do not mind, but I must ask permission of my father

before you take any books out of the house." Celia gestured towards the teacups on the table. "We have been so busy talking, I have not made the tea. And the water will be cold by the time we have visited the library. How vexing!"

Aurora could not find much sympathy. "Perhaps, when we come back," she suggested, "we may call for more."

"But I always have my tea *now*, after dinner!"

"Then let me go alone to the library." Aurora's heartbeat quickened. "I shall be better choosing books by myself, anyway. You can stay here and drink your tea."

This pleased Celia. "You are without doubt the cleverest and pleasantest girl I know," she declared, "and you must come and see me again tomorrow. My best friends are the Clarence sisters, in Brunswick Square. There are four of them, each as droll as you like. They will love you as I do, though you are much prettier than any of them. I am eager to introduce you!"

"I look forward to it," lied Aurora, who had no wish to be introduced to a family of four sisters, droll or otherwise. She stood up. "Does the library contain a volume of Shakespeare? I know my brother admires his work greatly."

Celia shrugged impatiently. "I do not know. You may look for one if you will."

"Very well," said Aurora, opening the parlour door. "I will be no more than a quarter of an hour."

Josiah and Joe Deede were still in the dining room. Aurora could hear their voices as she passed the door. In the library, she inspected one volume, then another, taking them to the table and leafing through them. When she was sure Celia had not decided to follow her after all, she placed a biography of Cardinal Wolsey on the narrow top of the writing desk, holding it there with one hand while she tried the hinged cover and the drawers with the other. All, as expected, were locked.

The table in the centre of the room had two drawers, for holding playing cards and chess pieces. Aurora had little hope that whoever had locked the writing desk would keep the key there, but she took Cardinal Wolsey to the table and opened them anyway. They did not contain any playing cards or chess pieces, but neither were they empty. One held writing implements – quills, penknife, wiper and ink – and sheets of paper ruled in lines after the fashion of schoolchildren. The other contained a Latin primer, much thumbed, and a rather newer copy of a handwriting practice book. As Aurora had suspected, this had been Edward's schoolroom.

Her hand shook as she felt at the back of each drawer, then peered underneath them, took them out of their casings and inspected the underside of the table itself. There was nothing there; no false bottoms or secret compartments, no hidden box or envelope. Nothing that could contain a small brass key.

She replaced the drawers as soundlessly as she could, and was straightening up when the door opened and Joe came in, followed more slowly by his father. Both looked surprised. "Miss Drayton!" Josiah the elder was the first to speak. "We thought you were upstairs with Celia."

"I was, sir," said Aurora apologetically. She had gone red, she knew. "But I expressed a wish to see the library. Celia kindly allowed me to browse here alone while she drank her tea."

"Tea is much more appetizing to my sister than

literature," observed Joe with a short laugh. "We despair of her, do we not, Father?"

"We do," said Josiah, his eyes on Aurora's face. "But you are a reader, Miss Drayton?"

"My brother is. I wonder if I may have your permission to borrow some books for him?"

"By all means," replied Josiah.

Aurora bobbed a curtsey. "Thank you. My brother will be most grateful. He is a quick reader – the books will be returned forthwith." She looked down at the book in her hand. "May I take this one? And this?" She picked up a volume of poems by Sir Walter Raleigh, the first book she had taken from the shelves, and opened it. "I see it is inscribed to someone called Elizabeth Francis," she observed. "If this lady is of significance to your family, of course I would not dream—"

"Take it! Take it, Miss Drayton!" Josiah Deede had turned on his heel and was striding out of the open door. "And come up and drink some tea, if you please!"

"I must go to my brother now, sir," she called after him, "so I will not take tea. But I will come and bid your daughter farewell." She turned to Joe, who gave a slight bow. "Your father is most kind."

Celia rose as Joe and Aurora entered the upstairs sitting room, where Josiah Deede was already seated. "Father says you are going, Aurora!" she cried accusingly.

"I must, I am afraid. My brother awaits me."

"But you shall come tomorrow, and visit the Clarences with me?"

Aurora looked at Josiah Deede. "I am invited by your daughter, sir…"

"If she wishes it, then it is so. You may come whenever you like." He gestured towards the window. "Indeed, why not pay a visit to Spring Gardens, while the weather is so pleasant? Is that not a good idea, Joe?"

Joe nodded, his eyes upon Aurora's face. "Will you come with us to Spring Gardens – shall we say on Saturday? If your brother will spare you, that is."

"Thank you, sir," said Aurora, curtseying. "I am sure he will."

Celia accompanied Aurora downstairs and embraced her as they parted on the doorstep. "I adore Spring Gardens, do you not?"

"I have never been there," confessed Aurora.

Celia stared. "How astonishing!"

"I have not lived in London long," Aurora reminded her. "I am sure I will find the gardens as delightful as people say they are. But now, I bid you goodbye. Please convey my thanks to your father and your … and Joe, for the hospitality I have received today."

She left Celia at the door, knowing she had coloured, and scolding herself for such weakness. But as she set off towards Floral Street her scolding turned to more serious self-rebuke. Would the spirit of her dear father ever forgive the lies she had told today, the false responses she had enacted and the pleasure she had felt in the company of a handsome – and fervently Catholic – man?

Praying silently, she set off with quickened steps for St James's Church.

A Skeleton in Her Dress

Aurora had assumed that she would wear her blue silk gown to visit Spring Gardens. But when she took it out of her trunk and shook out its creases, Edward dismayed her by telling her that the dress, at least in its present state, would not do.

"Spring Gardens is a pleasure-ground for the wealthy, but it is also a hunting-ground for professional ladies of low reputation," he declared. "You must resemble the former more than the latter."

"Impertinence!" she replied, but she had to acknowledge he was right.

There was not time to get a new dress made, but Edward gave her the money for a new front panel for the skirt of the old dress, ribbons for the back, and a new hat and gloves. "I must repay Richard when I can," he told her as he handed her the sovereigns. "Do not, I beg you, be extravagant."

She was as extravagant as a visit to Spring Gardens demanded. The necessity of avoiding anyone in the mantua-making business who might be known to her mother sent her south of the river to Lambeth, near the Gardens themselves, where Celia reported that she and her friends the Clarence sisters patronized a woman who did excellent work and did not overcharge.

The new silk panel, embroidered with tiny flowers and birds, matched the blue of the dress exactly. The ribbons, likewise, reflected the colour of Aurora's eyes. Standing in the mantua-maker's parlour before the tall looking-glass, Aurora was pulled this way and that as the woman drew up the back of the skirt and pinned the material into intricately gathered layers, ready for the ribbons to be sewn on. When the hat Aurora had already chosen from the milliner's next door was upon her head, and the new, lace-edged kid gloves on her hands, she allowed herself the luxury of noting that she was pretty enough to attract any man amongst the many hundreds who frequented Spring Gardens.

Aurora knew it was a wicked thought, but Joe was so handsome, and carried his sword and his opinions so boldly, she could not help observing to herself that he resembled the vision of her future husband far better than the man to whom she was actually married. The many hundreds of men did not matter; she wished to look pretty for Joe.

By Thursday evening the dress was finished, and Aurora put it on for Edward's inspection. "Lady of the night or daughter of the gentry?" she asked, posing.

She thought he would smile, but his face remained immobile. "Something in between."

"Perhaps if I wear a mask, as I did at the theatre?"

"No!" he protested. "In Spring Gardens a mask is the sign of a harlot."

Aurora felt admonished. She disliked it when Edward's

superior age and experience exposed her unworldliness. "Very well," she said stiffly.

He smiled then, and patted her shoulder. "You are to go to the Deedes' tomorrow, are you not?"

"I have been invited for dinner."

"You will be offered fish, no doubt," said Edward, still smiling, "as Catholics must abstain from meat on Fridays."

"I like fish," said Aurora blankly. "And it will be very finely cooked, you may be sure. No expense is spared at the Deedes' table."

A change came over Edward's face. Aurora was suddenly conscious of her careless words. "I did not mean—" she began, but he stopped her.

"Now," he said, "change out of this finery. I have something of great interest to show you."

When Aurora emerged from her chamber he was sitting at the table. As usual, Mary had not yet collected the breakfast dishes; Edward had pushed them aside. He motioned to the other chair, and when Aurora was seated he held up the key which opened the outer door of their rooms. "What do you notice about this key?" he asked her.

Aurora frowned at it. It looked the same as every door key she had ever seen. Fashioned from iron, with a ring at the end, a plain shaft and a head with a pattern cut out, like teeth. "It is an ordinary key," she said helplessly.

"And what about this one?" He held up another door key, which looked the same except that it was plainer.

"That one fits a different lock?" hazarded Aurora, feeling like a child interrogated by its tutor.

Edward lowered his voice. "It will fit almost any lock. It is a skeleton key."

He laid the keys beside each other on the table. "See, our key has several teeth, and a depression at the end that fits into a pin."

Aurora inspected the end of the key. True enough, it was hollowed out. "I have never noticed that before," she confessed.

"All keys of this type have that depression. And all have a number of teeth, which fit into notches inside the lock. But this one, the skeleton, has the depression at the end, but only one tooth, at the top. That is why it is known as a skeleton key – it has not the flesh of the true key."

Aurora strove to understand. "So, inside the keyhole, these teeth make the lock turn, which unlatches the door. Is that correct?"

"Quite correct," nodded Edward.

"So when you put the skeleton key in the keyhole, how can it work, if it has no teeth?"

"Because it *bypasses* the notches the teeth are supposed to fit into, but latches on to the pin at the end. When you turn the key, the pin and the barrel of the lock turn, and the door opens."

Aurora stared at the skeleton key. "So can anyone make a key like this, which will fit any door lock, by filing off the other teeth?" she asked incredulously.

"That is, in theory, true," said Edward. "Though in practice it does take some skill. But that is why such locks only appear on things of little value."

Aurora nodded. "Such as our door." She considered for a moment. "Or a writing desk?"

"Exactly. At the first opportunity, try this key in the lock of that cabinet in the library. My family has no such piece of furniture; Josiah Deede must have brought it from Tavistock Street, so everything in it must belong to him or his children. No doubt he carries the key everywhere he goes, but has not added to the security of the desk by padlocking it. Perhaps his children also have keys."

"I must be prepared to find nothing of interest," observed Aurora despondently. "His private papers are more likely locked up in his office, or in a chest in his bedroom."

"Perhaps." Edward watched her turning the key round and round in her fingers. "But he regulates carefully who enters his house, and is very unlikely to suspect his daughter's new friend. With a little luck this key will reveal something."

"If it works," said Aurora, scrutinizing the key.

"It will work. It was made by a craftsman."

They regarded each other, Aurora with a frown and Edward with the hint of a smile. "I will ask no more questions," she told him, weighing the key in her palm, "as it is plain I will get no answers. And I will keep this in a very safe place until I am called upon to use it." She slipped the key down the top of her bodice. It felt cold against her skin, but secure against any intruder. "I promise you, Edward, I am as eager as you are for this deception to be over. I *will* find the truth."

When she arrived at Mill Street on Friday, Joe Deede was from home. He had also been out on Wednesday, when she had accompanied Celia to Brunswick Square to take tea with the Clarences. Four days had now passed since she had last been in his company.

It seemed that she was expected to act as Celia's friend,

ready with flattery and gratitude whenever Miss Deede desired it, pandering to the girl's vanity, self-centredness and ignorance, and that of her acquaintances. Celia treated Aurora pleasantly, but the notion that she considered her as a new distraction, to be discarded when another came along, was never far from Aurora's mind. She told herself that was what rich girls were like; the Clarence sisters had displayed the same attitude. But this thought did not make it easy to bear so much of Celia's company when she would have preferred a little more of Joe's.

"Where does your brother go, that he spends so many hours from home?" she asked Celia nervously, fearing to incur more accusations that she must be madly in love with him.

But Celia responded with affectionately scornful laughter. "White's, of course! Where he sits with his friends and chews the world to pieces, arguing and pontificating, as stubborn as a dog with a tough old bone. I thank God I can have no part of it."

Aurora did not acquiesce. Coffee houses, with their unrestricted gathering of men and minds, had always seemed attractive to her. Celia might be glad that women were forbidden to enter them, but Aurora had far rather accompany Joe to White's than sit in the parlour with his sister.

Her mission today, however, was to engineer enough time alone in the library to attempt to unlock the cabinet. To that end, she had brought back the books she had borrowed. She now put them on the worktable and handed Celia a note. "My brother thanks you for the loan of the books," she said, "and sends you this."

Celia made a great show of bashful astonishment as

she unfolded the letter. "What a delightful hand!" she exclaimed as she read it. It was Aurora's hand, heavily disguised, though the words had been dictated by Edward. "And equally delightful sentiments." She looked up from the letter. "What a pity your brother is so ill. I am sure he is very charming."

Aurora smiled. "A charming Protestant?"

Celia shrugged her slim shoulders. "I suppose so." She sighed, letting the letter fall into her lap. "But you know, Aurora, I sometimes wonder if I will *ever* be permitted to have a suitor. Father is so strict."

"You are young," said Aurora soothingly. "There is plenty of time for a young man of the Catholic faith, whom your father considers suitable, to turn up."

Celia did not look convinced. "I hope so. But you are younger than I, and you have got Joe."

"I have not 'got' Joe!" protested Aurora. "I have met him but once!"

Celia responded with a knowing look. "Twice, actually." She folded up the letter and put it in her workbox. Aurora wondered if she would reread it later, letting loose her dreams of the non-existent Edward Drayton. Guilt swept over her. Spying on Josiah Deede might suit her nature, as Edward had pointed out, but this deception of his artless daughter did not.

"May I borrow some more books for Edward?" she asked.

"Of course." Celia laughed briefly. "Any man who writes such an elegant letter may borrow as many books as he chooses!"

"Thank you," said Aurora, standing up. "I will take

these back down and bring some more up, and then, perhaps, we could go for a walk? It is another beautiful day." She thought quickly. "While I am downstairs I could tell Harrison to bring our cloaks, and save you calling him. You have better things to do than run after servants."

Celia was satisfied with any suggestion that implied she was important. "You are so good, my dear. Always thinking of me." She drew her workbox towards her. "I will get on with my work."

Or read that infernal letter again, thought Aurora. "I will not be many minutes," she assured the girl, and, with the books under her arm and the skeleton key nestling between her breasts, she walked quickly downstairs to the library and closed the door behind her.

She put the books on the table. Taking the key from her bodice, she slid it into the keyhole in the front of the writing desk, pushed it as far as it would go, and tried to turn it. Nothing happened. She tried withdrawing it a little; she tried turning it the other way; she tried lifting it as she turned, then depressing it. But it would not budge, and the desk remained locked. Frustrated, Aurora tried the key in the lock that secured the top drawer, immediately under the hinged front of the desk. To her amazement it slipped in as if made for the purpose, and turned as if newly oiled.

There was nothing of interest in the drawer. Writing paper, sealing wax, a dusty collection of old quills, a long-unused snuffbox right at the back. The key also unlocked the next drawer, and the bottom one. In none of them was anything that could be remotely connected with Henry Francis, or indeed with anyone. No letters, documents, money, forged wills, incriminating objects of any kind.

It was as she had said to Edward: Josiah Deede kept his important papers locked up in his office, under a locking system less easily breached.

Why would the front of the desk not open, though? She stood there frowning, and a dim memory came to her of something her father had once told her. "Hidden in plain sight" was the expression he had used to describe to her and an equally fascinated Flora how God created certain animals with clever markings so that they could hide from predators. A speckled bird in a laurel bush, a stoat in the snow – no one could see them although they were there all the time.

She felt gingerly at the back of the top drawer, moving the paper, the stick of sealing wax and the quills out of the way. When she tried to do the same to the snuffbox, however, she found she could not. It was fixed, either to the bottom or the back of the drawer. Her body tensing, she tried to pull the entire drawer out of its casing. It would not move. She had heard of this: cleverly made hiding places in seemingly innocent pieces of furniture. Just as with the speckled bird and the white-coated stoat, someone was sure that what they had hidden could not be seen – unless a more determined predator than usual should be looking.

Carefully, she pushed, pulled, and eventually twisted the small wooden box. It was not a box at all; it had never held snuff. It was actually a turning mechanism that opened the back of the drawer. She knelt down and felt with trembling fingers for a further mechanism – a lever, a key, something she was sure was there, which would lead the way to the locked upper compartment of the desk.

Suddenly, she had it. She was not sure how, but her

exploring hand had touched something that had operated some kind of spring. To Aurora's utter surprise, the entire hinged front of the desk opened about an inch, remaining propped there, ready to be lowered from the outside. She inspected the keyhole. It was false, a mere ornament covering a smooth hole with no pin for the skeleton key to attach itself to. The upper part of the desk could only be unlocked by someone who knew how.

This was Josiah Deede's personal hiding place.

She lowered the front of the cabinet. As expected, behind it she saw many compartments and small drawers. The compartments were all empty. Aurora opened each drawer. Empty too. But she was convinced that no one would go to this much trouble to conceal something unless there was something to conceal. She felt at the back of each drawer, prodding the corners, searching for another spring. And at last, on the fourth drawer she tried, she found it. The back of the drawer tipped forwards, and Aurora's fingers closed around a folded piece of paper, apparently a letter, with a broken seal.

How long had she been in the library? Celia must not come downstairs looking for her. Aurora thrust the letter as far down her bodice as her corset would allow, replaced the back of the drawer, shut the drawer, and pulled up the hinged front with its false keyhole. She had just done this – her hand was still on the top corner of the cabinet – when she heard the door open behind her.

"Why, Aurora, what are you doing?" came Celia's bewildered voice.

Aurora turned. Joe had followed his sister into the room, and was flicking his eyes from Aurora, to the bookshelves, to the table, to the cabinet. He was not bewildered like Celia; he was suspicious. Aurora searched fruitlessly for an explanation of her position. Then, as smoothly as a prompt from the side of the stage, her mother's voice floated into her head. "When all else fails, girls, swoon."

She let out a quiet shriek and fell to the floor. Luckily her hat came off, or she would have squashed it. For authenticity, she had to fall quite hard, and the stone floor of the library, uncarpeted where she stood, was not forgiving. Her hip bone would have a bruise tomorrow.

She heard her name cried out in both a female and a male voice, and then Celia's alone, very agitated, instructing her brother to carry Aurora to a chair. "Harrison!" she called down the passage to the kitchen. "Bring water! Miss Drayton is not well!"

Aurora felt herself lifted and held against Joe Deede's body. He set her down, and she heard the man-servant's footsteps on the flagstones. Harrison must have given his mistress a glass of water, as a wetted handkerchief soon dabbed Aurora's forehead and a feminine hand took hers.

"How pale she looks!" observed Celia. "She must be worn out, poor thing. Watching her brother's condition worsen day by day must be a terrible strain. And you know, Joe, they have no mother or father!"

Joe did not reply. Aurora kept her eyes closed, trying not to think too hard about what his expression might be like and trying to fathom the situation in which she found herself.

It was surely impossible that these two concerned young people had been privy to their father's crime. It must be Josiah Deede – the intolerant convert, the disloyal friend and the possessor of a very sophisticated hiding place – who alone was guilty.

The paper she had found must be of great importance to him. It was bound to reveal something. She would carry it back to Edward like a trophy. And perhaps, long before the allotted month had passed, she would be free.

"Oh!" she exclaimed, opening her eyes. She was sitting on a wooden chair, placed against the wall of the library. Joe sat next to her, close enough for her to feel his warmth and smell the familiar odour of wig hair.

"You fainted," said Celia, looking very relieved. "I wondered why you were leaning on the writing desk. You must have suddenly weakened, and were unable to support yourself. If only Joe had caught you before you fell!"

"Such foolishness," said Aurora. "I am so sorry."

"Not foolishness." Joe took the glass of water from Celia and handed it to Aurora. "Fatigue. Here, sip this."

"And then you must come up and have some tea," added Celia. "I hope you are not going to be ill, for we are going to Spring Gardens tomorrow."

"You are very kind." Aurora sat up and looked around for her hat. "I shall be recovered in no time."

Celia handed her the hat. "Are you well enough to stand? Lean on Joe."

They made their way upstairs slowly, Aurora hanging on Joe's arm. As he settled her in his father's chair with her feet on the footstool, she saw on his face the kind of affectionate possessiveness she had last seen on Edward's when he had kissed her at the wedding and Eleanora had started to cry. "Thank you, Joe," she said.

There was a timid knock, and Missy, the pretty, neatly

clad housemaid, came in with a laden tea tray. She was followed by Harrison bearing a steaming kettle, which he placed on a trivet in the hearth. When the servants had quitted the room, Celia used a small key she wore on a chain about her waist to open the tea casket. Aurora watched, thinking of the pride of place her mother's tea casket – a box inlaid with ivory – took in the parlour at home. Tea was too expensive to be left in the kitchen for servants to steal.

Celia made the tea and gave the cups to Joe to distribute. He set Aurora's at her elbow, where she watched its spiral of steam disperse in the sunny room for a few moments before she picked it up.

"When I have drunk my tea I must go," she told them decisively. "I do not think I can eat dinner. I had better rest at home."

"Then you must allow me to accompany you in the carriage as far as, say, Charing Cross," said Joe. "You cannot walk all the way."

If her fainting fit were to seem genuine, there was no possibility of protest. "Very well, sir."

The three of them chatted idly while they finished their tea. Aurora could feel the edges of the folded paper inside her bodice, pressing into her flesh. This delay caused by the drinking of tea would at least be offset by a carriage ride for more than half the distance back to the lodging rooms. She had promised Edward she would be back as soon after dinner as she could. He would be surprised to see her returned so early. And hopefully, he would be pleased with her morning's work.

Harrison was told to order the carriage. Aurora collected her hat and kissed Celia, who grasped her hand.

"What about your brother's books?" she asked. "They must still be in the library. Joe, collect them on your way out."

"There is no need," Aurora assured her. "I had not progressed very far in choosing books when I began to feel faint. I will select some on my next visit."

"But your next visit is tomorrow!" protested Celia. "We are going to Spring Gardens!"

Aurora could see Celia was not to be denied. The girl was hoping, no doubt, for another communication from Edward Drayton. Turning to Joe, Aurora smiled encouragingly. "Your sister is so kind. Perhaps you might choose some books you think my brother would like, and I can collect them tomorrow evening?"

"It would be an honour," said Joe.

It was hot in the carriage, even with the windows down. Aurora fanned herself all the way to Charing Cross, trying to calm her agitation. The piece of paper must have slipped further down inside her dress. She could no longer feel it there, but could not check for it with Joe sitting only inches away from her. She prayed it had not fallen out.

When the carriage stopped, Joe alighted and handed her out. Before he let go of her hand he raised it to his lips, bestowing a kiss upon her gloved fingers. "Until tomorrow."

"At seven o'clock." Aurora smiled. "Goodbye, and thank you again."

He bowed, and climbed back into the carriage. "Fare thee well, Aurora."

She watched until the carriage was out of sight. Even though she was convinced it would not have mattered if Joe had seen where she went, she had assured Edward that she would be zealously careful, and she must keep that promise.

Turning away from the road, she slipped into the shadow of the buildings and felt for the paper. It was still there. She wavered a moment, indecisive, wondering whether to withdraw it and read it. Then she sighed and set off once more for Samuel Marshall's bookshop.

The attic was deserted. Aurora stood at the open door with her hand on the latch, unable to contain her irritation.

Edward had left no note on the table. She checked her own room. Nothing. She went to the top of the stairs and called. "Mary! Mary, do not pretend you cannot hear me!"

After a few minutes Mary shuffled up the lower flight and waited, looking up sullenly.

"Tell me, when did Mr Drayton go out?" asked Aurora.

"Cannot say, 'm."

"Is Mr Marshall in?"

"Yes, 'm."

"Thank you. That is all."

Aurora went back into her own room. The glass confirmed that she looked as anxious as she felt. The flesh of her face was as lifeless as clay. She pinched blood into her cheeks, but could do nothing to disguise the dullness of her eyes, nor the smudges beneath them. She pulled her hat brim forward and set off down the stairs.

A light showed under Samuel Marshall's door; he must have lately finished his dinner. Perhaps he had spoken to Edward earlier in the shop, and might know where he had gone. Aurora set an expression of polite enquiry on her face, and knocked.

"Come in!"

When she opened the door she was met by the sight of

Mr Marshall – his round face bathed in delight, his gouty foot supported on a stool – sitting at a table weighted with books, ale tankards and the remains of a platter of bread and cheese. On the other side of the table, smiling sheepishly, sat Edward.

"My dear Miss Drayton!" The landlord indicated with his walking stick a chair in the corner. "Draw up that chair and partake of some cheese, if you will. And there is some ale left in the pitcher."

There could not have been much. Mr Marshall, gout or no gout, was very intoxicated. Edward, who was less so, raised the pitcher. "Empty."

"Pray do not trouble yourself, sir," said Aurora to Mr Marshall with a curtsey. "I have a private message for Mr Drayton that will not wait."

Mr Marshall raised his eyebrows at Edward. "A private message?" He looked back at Aurora. "I trust it is not bad news?"

"It is of great import," said Aurora.

"Then I will come at once," said Edward. He rose and picked up his hat. It was the green one. She looked at it, remembering how the sunlight from her mother's drawing-room windows had fallen upon it.

"I bid you good day, Edward," said Samuel Marshall, nodding in the studied way of the inebriated. "You and your sister both."

"Good day, sir," said Edward, "and many thanks for your hospitality."

"Come down after dinner whenever you like."

Edward bowed, and they left the room. "I was very happy in there," he told Aurora. "What can be of such great import that you pluck me from such good company?"

"I cannot tell you here, on the stairs. I have come straight from Mill Street."

Edward frowned. "Then they eat their fish *very* early."

"I did not stay for dinner."

"Why, then, you should have partaken of some cheese when Mr Marshall offered it!" he exclaimed. "There is no food up here. I have eaten it all."

"Edward!" Aurora dragged him into the attic room and shut the door. "I have brought something from Mill Street. I pray you, attend."

"Very well, I will attend. But may I make myself comfortable first?"

He removed his coat and wig and put on his well-worn grey worsted house robe, that garment so despised by Joe Deede. He placed his sword, its belt and holder still attached, against the wall. The table was spread with the remains of their breakfast, which Mary had again neglected to clear. The window was too small to admit much sunlight, and the room was gloomy. Removing her hat and gloves, Aurora sat down on the edge of Edward's bed. "Would you light a candle, please?" she asked. "I wish you to read something."

He took the tinderbox from the mantelpiece, lit a candle and placed it in the centre of the table. Then he sat down, sprawling in the chair with his elbow on the table. He had drunk enough wine for his eyes to have a wayward, abandoned look. "So, faithful accomplice, what is your report?" he asked.

Aurora told him about the dummy keyhole, the snuffbox, the levers and mechanisms, the false drawer backs, the folded paper. He listened without interruption, not looking at her, but studying, as he often did, the candle flame. It was too far away to light much of his face, but Aurora watched his eyes become increasingly concerned as she talked.

"Please, let me see the paper," he demanded as soon as she ceased.

She drew it from her bodice. He unfolded it, held it close to the candle and read it quickly. His expression remained passive, though tinged now with sorrow.

"Is it a letter?" she asked.

"It is." He cast it upon the bed beside her. "Read it."

Aurora picked up the letter. It was dated the fifteenth of February, 1698, more than two years ago, and was addressed to Josiah Deede in a neat hand.

Mill Street, Mayfair

My honoured friend,

I hope you will forgive this timely reminder of your promise. Our mutual friend will be at his post at seven o'clock this Friday evening, in the usual place. I have no doubt you will fulfil your obligation, but may I prevail upon you to make that obligation a little larger than last month? I find I am no longer able to keep the costs of this venture at the level they once were. Thirty-five shillings should be sufficient. I hope I shall not have to prevail upon you again for a further increase, though of course this cannot be guaranteed.

If you wish a return upon your investment, as a businessman you will understand my request. I will endeavour as usual to obtain for you the very best return.

I am, sir, indebted to you for your continued generosity,
H. F.

Aurora was so shocked that her breath disappeared. She felt as if an invisible hand with the strength of a giant had struck a blow to her chest. It was the letter of a blackmailer. A blackmailer who signed himself "H. F."

Her throat had dried. She swallowed, watching Edward. No indignation or anger had come into his eyes.

"Edward, this letter is from your father," she said, bewildered.

"It is not." His voice was full of contempt.

"But the initials—"

"It is a forgery."

Aurora looked again at the letter, and back at Edward. "You must face the truth," she told him gently. "The evidence is here before your eyes."

"The truth? I will tell you the truth!" He leaned towards her, his expression alert, with no trace of intoxication. "Consider this," he began in a low, patient voice: "My father was a healthy man of fifty-one when he died. That is to say, his organs were sound and he had no fatal disease. Of course men may suffer diseases that do not kill yet inflict great discomfort upon their victim. Look at poor Samuel Marshall, almost crippled with gout."

Aurora did not understand. "But what has this to do with the letter?"

"I beg you, forbear. My father suffered greatly from rheumatism. By the time I was fifteen, his hands were so gnarled and painful it had become impossible for him to write his own letters. At the palace he had an amanuensis to do it for him; at home he relied upon me. All he could do was scrawl his signature – the signature that appears on the altered will."

Aurora's heart sank. "So you are saying that he could not have written this letter two years ago?"

"Nor at any other time in the ten years before his death."

Resentment crept over her. She felt an irrational desire to stamp her foot. "Why should I believe you?" she demanded. "Short of exhuming your father's body and showing me his skeleton, you have no proof!"

"Then you must take my word as a man of honour," he told her steadily.

"And you must take *my* word that this letter is the key to your father's death!" She picked up the letter and shook it. "The contents of this show that it was not the only blackmail letter Josiah Deede received. He must have paid a great deal of money to the sender, burning the letters, saving only this one against the day, perhaps, when he could bring his tormentor to justice."

Edward nodded in agreement. "That is plausible, certainly. But since the letter is forged, and my father was not his tormentor, who was?"

Aurora thought for a moment, frowning. "Someone who knew something about Josiah Deede that he does not want made public," she reasoned. "I wish we knew what it could be! But whoever the blackmailer was, they wanted Deede to believe his tormentor was Henry Francis. "

Edward's face was again sorrowful, again immovable. He did not speak.

"Perhaps the blackmailer wanted your father dead all along," ventured Aurora, "so they engineered a way to incite Josiah Deede to murder him. The two men were already enemies, after all. Blackmail would surely drive the final wedge between them."

She paused. She had thought of something else, and looked carefully at Edward, to watch his response as she voiced it. "Or … will you consider the possibility that your father was *guilty*? You said you used to act as his amanuensis, so why could not someone else do the same?"

"Because my father was not a blackmailer!" Edward slapped his hand down on the table so hard Aurora jumped. "Because the letter is written in a hand attempting to mimic his! The writer does not *know* my father suffered from rheumatism. This person has copied his handwriting from some document written many years ago."

He sat back, his fingers striking the edge of the table repeatedly, his face filled with concentration. "You are correct, it is someone who knows Josiah Deede's secret. If we can find out what that secret is, we will, as you say, find the key to my father's death." His black eyes roved restlessly over Aurora's face. "You have done very well today, but there is much more to do if we are to expose Josiah Deede's villainy, and my father's innocence, before the world. "

Aurora let her head drop forward, resting her forehead on her fingers. She felt intolerably weary, as if she had struggled through a quagmire, only to find herself confronted with quicksand.

"For a moment I thought I would be able to go home," she confessed miserably. "I thought my promise to you had been fulfilled. The letter seemed to show that your father was a heartless criminal, who disinherited you and left his fortune to Josiah Deede in order to make his peace with God." She sighed, a juddering, disappointed sigh. "And now," she went on, "I find I have to stay in this horrible place for Lord knows how long, and not see my sisters, and … and everything has gone wrong!"

Unable to hold her head up any longer, she lay down on Edward's pillow and closed her eyes. She thought about the little shop with its shelves of silks and damasks, the measuring tapes, the cutting table, the snippets of material on the floor. She pictured her mother sitting on the high stool, humming softly as she held a newly ruffled cuff to the light. She thought about Eleanora curled up in the corner of the parlour window seat, reading by candlelight when she should have been in bed, because Mrs Eversedge did not allow her youngest daughter candles in the bedroom. Aurora thought about Flora, trimming and retrimming her gowns and hats, turning this way and that in front of the looking-glass, making a *moue* with her lips, smiling and chattering to whomever would listen. Dear Flora.

Thinking about these things made Aurora's heart heavy. But when she opened her eyes she saw that Edward's own melancholy had increased. He hunched his shoulders, twisted his hands together until he noticed what he was doing, then stopped. He released air slowly down his nose, his lips in a narrow line.

"You are right," he said. "I have asked too much of you. I will take you home and continue my quest alone."

There was no doubt that Aurora would very much like to be Miss Eversedge again. But as she lay there against the pillows, her gaze resting on her husband, she realized with a rush of compassion that he did, indeed, love her. If she stripped away the guile, the art, the trickery and bargain-making of their first encounter, what was left was love. His remorse was real. But so was her belief, taught to her by her father, in the uncompromising pursuit of a just cause.

"Edward," she said decisively, "listen to me. There is no question of my returning home. I will go to Spring Gardens with the Deedes tomorrow. I will play my part as Aurora Drayton and do everything I can to discover either the secret, or the identity of the blackmailer. Not one of the Deedes connects Aurora Drayton with either Henry or Edward Francis, and that is her most powerful weapon."

Edward was silent for a long time. Aurora waited, watching the yellowish light strike the prominent bones of his face. Then his shoulders went down a little. He blinked and ran his hand over his chin, rubbing his beard as Aurora had often seen men do when they have not shaved for many hours.

"Very well," he said with an almost-invisible nod. "I must leave it up to God to keep you safe."

Aurora reached for her hat. "I will go and rest now," she said, feeling, for some reason, awkward. But she could not think of anything to add that would take the awkwardness away.

They looked at each other. Edward's face was inscrutable again; Aurora could not tell what was in his mind or his heart. Then he broke his gaze and seemed to collect himself. "I am to meet Richard at Will's Coffee House tomorrow evening," he said in a brighter tone. "He has a letter from Hartford House for you."

"Then I thank him for that."

Edward's calm expression did not change. "When I see him, I will congratulate him on the success of the skeleton key, for he is the craftsman who made it."

It was at that moment that the world fell in on Aurora.

She sat up so suddenly, and with such horror on her face, that Edward rose and came to the bedside, very concerned. "What is it?" He gripped her hand. "Are you unwell?"

"Oh, dear God!" she cried. "Oh, Edward, I have left the skeleton key in the writing desk!"

His mouth opened, and he blinked rapidly, but he did not speak.

"Celia and Joe came in just as I had closed the lid of the desk," continued Aurora. "I had no business being near it, so I pretended to swoon. Dear God, my stupidity has undone us!"

"But the key is probably still there, unnoticed," he offered.

Aurora shook her head desperately. "There is worse, I am afraid. Celia reminded me I had not taken books for my brother, so I asked Joe if he would select some for me to collect tomorrow." She looked at Edward, then looked away again and withdrew her hand. She could not bear the admonishment that was bound to come. "Joe will go to the library and find the key, and all will be lost!"

"Not necessarily."

She turned her head. Edward's eyes were fixed on hers, full of concentration. "You have given yourself the opportunity to enter the library tomorrow," he observed. "When you collect the books, you can also collect the key. If Joe Deede has seen it, he has no reason not to think his father left it there. He will not connect it with Miss Drayton. As long as Josiah Deede himself does not discover it, we are safe."

Aurora chewed her lower lip, trying to believe him, her imagination galloping. "Supposing Joe removes the key, assuming it to be his father's, and takes it to Josiah?"

"Josiah Deede is a clever and devious man," he said seriously, "but if his suspicions are aroused we must be cleverer and more devious. Above all, we must not under-estimate him."

He stood up, snuffed the candle and put on his coat and wig. "I am going out. Do not unlock the door. I will return soon, and bring food."

Aurora rose too, and stood by his side. "Edward…"

He put on his hat. Beneath its brim, his eyes were black and inscrutable again.

"I am sorry," she said, looking at the floorboards. "For doubting your father's innocence, and for forgetting the key."

"Very well, but I am not sorry at all."

She raised her head. "What do you mean?"

"Aurora, the crisis has come. By tomorrow evening we will know whether Josiah Deede will show his true colours. The question then remains: when will he strike?"

Double-dealer

When Harrison opened the door Aurora walked past him before he could object. "Mr Joe arranged for me to collect some books when we return from Spring Gardens this evening," she said, opening the library door. "I wish to inspect them."

"Very well, Miss," said Harrison with a bow. "I will inform him and Miss Celia that you are here."

Aurora could already hear Celia's excited voice from the landing. She crossed the library to the cabinet; the key was where she had left it. Faint with relief, she removed it with shaking fingers and put it into the deep pocket in the seam of her dress. Then, labouring to draw sufficient breath, she seized the pile of books that lay on the table and opened the first one.

"Aurora!" trilled Celia, entering in a rustle of silk and holding out her hands. "How fine you look!"

"Thank you," replied Aurora. Her breathing had almost returned to normal. She put down the books and smiled amiably. "But not as fine as you."

Celia was wearing a gown embroidered in shimmering

shades of brown and silver. From her corseted bosom to her trailing hem, from the lace on her sleeves to the silver adornments on her shoes, she sparkled with wealth and newness. "Oh, nonsense! Your hair is *beautiful*. And is that a new hat?"

Aurora had spent a long time attending to her hair, cursing the cramped quarters and lack of a dressing-table, and wishing Hester were there to help her. But the result had brought the unsmiling remark from Edward that the style was surprisingly flattering, considering it was also fashionable.

"If Joe is not in love with you already, he will be before this evening is over!" smirked Celia. "Your beauty will attract the attention of all who pass by!"

Aurora fervently hoped not. *She* might never have set foot in Spring Gardens before, the admission price being too high for Mrs Eversedge's means, but any one of her parents' acquaintance could be amongst its visitors this evening. If she should see someone she recognized, she would have to rely on the unexpectedness of the company she was in, the stylishness of her coiffure and the wide brim of her hat to persuade them that she was not Catherine Eversedge's eldest girl after all, but merely a young woman who bore some resemblance to her.

She turned as the door opened and Joe came in, smiling and wishing her good evening. In place of his usual worsted coat he wore a dark suit edged with gold. From its wide sleeves hung ruffles adorned with lace, and his waistcoat was embroidered as luxuriantly as any Aurora and her sisters had observed on titled gentlemen in St James's Park. The suit, like Celia's gown, looked newly delivered from the tailor.

"I trust you are recovered?" he asked. As he made a

small bow, his admiring eyes remained on Aurora's face. She had to struggle to control her feelings; she was flattered, because she was made of human flesh and could not help it. But blushing like a maidservant would not do.

"Quite recovered, I thank you, sir," she told him. "And I thank you also for looking out these books for my brother. I will take them home later, when I have explored every part of Spring Gardens."

He gave a short laugh, holding out his arm. "You may *begin* to explore the Gardens tonight, Aurora, but several more visits will be necessary before you can say you have explored *every part*. The area is perhaps larger than you are aware."

"Perhaps," agreed Aurora, taking his arm. "But I would still like to see it all."

"Then I look forward to many more visits there in your company," said Joe politely, with another slight bow.

Aurora did not speak; her neck and cheeks felt hot.

"Joe has been there many times." Celia threw Aurora a knowing look as she took her brother's other arm. "He knows there are alleys so well hidden a man and a woman may very easily separate themselves from their companions!"

The Thames lay, silvered by the evening sun, between the landing stage where the carriage deposited them and Spring Gardens. Aurora had been up and down the river on boats before; it was a swift means of London travel, especially in winter when mud or flood made some streets impassable. But she had never been on a boat like the one that ferried her and her fellow pleasure-seekers to the gates of the Gardens.

Many of the passengers seemed the worse for drink,

and those who were not might as well have been, from the high state of their excitement. There was much flirtatious behaviour; Aurora's face was examined by so many strange men she pretended to object to the river breeze, and put up her fan. Celia seemed not to mind who looked at her own countenance. Neither did Joe seem averse to ogling the elegant young women clustered on the benches, or standing in the prow holding their hats on and laughing.

This wealthy society into which she had blundered, Aurora thought ruefully, had lessons for her. Like the Theatre Royal, another place of entertainment to which the admission price was set to exclude the lower orders, Spring Gardens lent itself to vanity, intoxication and a loosening of propriety. If she were to pretend to be, or even one day actually become, a member of this society, she must revise her own conduct.

Joe was in high spirits. "Supper begins at nine o'clock," he told Aurora as they showed their tickets and entered the gates. "Before we sit down to sup, there will be music. Perhaps even a singer. I confess I do like a singer, especially a lady, do you not?"

Aurora did not reply. She was barely conscious that he had spoken. How she wished that Flora and Eleanora could see this! It was scarcely believable that London streets and the river Thames were only yards from where she stood. It was as if she had entered fairyland.

Before her stretched a long walkway edged with trees hung with lanterns. To the left and right spread alleys between banks of foliage – secret, overarching and utterly charming. There was a place for an orchestra and pavilions where food and drink could be purchased. Beneath an awning, tables were laid out for the grand supper. Everything sparkled – the evening sunlight between the branches, the lights, the decorations, the finery of the ladies and gentlemen. Everywhere Aurora looked there were people strolling, laughing, chattering, meeting old acquaintances and being introduced to new ones. There was much curtseying, fluttering of fans and tossing of heads amongst the young ladies, and much bowing, strutting and banter amongst the young men. To Aurora it seemed like a dance performed by hundreds of lavishly dressed dancers, moving to an accompaniment of orchestral music, and washed by waves of many other sounds.

"Astonishing!" she breathed. "I had no idea!"

"Spring Gardens are the envy of the world," Celia told her importantly.

"Of course." They had begun to make their way along the main walkway. It was slow-going, such were the crowds, but Aurora did not mind. "I do not think I have ever seen a more charming place!"

"And here is a charming person," said Joe drily. "Someone you know, Aurora."

Approaching them, waving her fan and showing all her teeth, was Mrs Fellowes. "My *dears*! And Miss Drayton too! What luck!"

Joe bowed and waited while Aurora and his sister curtseyed to the older woman. Then, smiling, he asked, "You are without Mr Fellowes this evening, madam?"

"I am," sighed Mrs Fellowes. "He says he is tired of the Gardens. But I will never tire of them, and I told him as much. 'Go alone, then,' said he, so I took him at his word. Though I have my friend Mrs Partridge with me."

She scanned the crowd. "She is probably getting us some refreshment. She will not wait until nine o'clock, I fear."

"Then I am of Mrs Partridge's mind exactly," said Joe gallantly, turning to Aurora. "Will you join me in seeking some refreshment?"

Aurora accepted, aware at the corner of her vision that Mrs Fellowes and Celia were exchanging meaningful glances.

"Let us step this way," said Joe, offering his arm.

"What about you, Celia? " asked Aurora.

Celia smiled archly. "I shall go with Mrs Fellowes to find Mrs Partridge, who is always full of *interesting* stories. We shall all meet again for supper. Fare you well."

Joe bought two glasses of wine. With one in each hand, he led Aurora along a twisting path, screened from all the others, where they came upon a large tree with a wooden bench set around it. The bench was already partly occupied, for here was an opportunity for girls and their admirers to escape their chaperones.

Aurora sat down and took a sip of wine. "Delicious!"

"It should be, considering what I was charged for it." Smiling amiably, Joe flipped the back of his coat as he sat. Aurora was reminded of how Edward had done the same with the coat of his green suit when he had sat down in her mother's parlour on that momentous day. Rich men – even Joe, who usually dressed so plainly – did not like to crease their fine clothes any more than rich women did. Aurora's heart quailed at the thought that she had already failed to conduct herself like a rich woman; she was sitting on her new, expensive, neatly ironed ribbons.

"I suppose the patrons of Spring Gardens must pay

what is asked, once they have entered," she observed. "The prices are no doubt agreed amongst the traders."

Joe raised his glass. "So you are a businesswoman now, as well as everything else, are you?"

Aurora's heart gave a thud. She tapped her fan gently against her chin, pretending to ponder modestly upon his words. "Everything else? Whatever can you mean?"

Amusement gleamed in his eyes. Blue eyes, but a greyer blue than Aurora's own, which her father used to say were the colour of God's own canopy. "You are clever," he began, "and fair of face and figure, and" – he sipped his wine – "you are a good sister to your brother, as well as a most excellent companion to Celia." He became more serious. "Indeed, I have become concerned that my sister is demanding your company too much. Does your brother not wish you to be more often at home?"

"Not at all." Aurora's heartbeat had subdued itself, but she nevertheless opened her fan and put it up. If Joe could see her whole face, he might discern the falsehoods to come. "My brother spends many hours writing and reading, during which I can be of no use to him. Thanks to your generosity, he has a plentiful supply of books, and as he cannot walk far, he is as happy as is possible on his couch. And the servant is there to tend to his needs."

Joe nodded. "But does he not wish for conversation with you? One cannot talk to a servant."

"Oh, we converse a great deal," Aurora assured him. "I am usually at home in the evenings. Tonight is an exception."

"And the night we met you at Drury Lane? Was that an exception too?"

Aurora fanned herself vigorously. She knew she must

provide a plausible explanation for her apparent neglect of a dying man. "Joe," she said, putting down the fan and regarding him as seriously as he was regarding her, "as I have confessed, my brother is in hiding from creditors. He cannot make his whereabouts public. Neither can he go out, though he is too ill to do so, anyway. For myself, I cannot do the first thing, but I *can* do the second, and I have his blessing to do so. He knows I crave the company of others, and being so lately arrived in London, our friends are far away."

Joe nodded. He seemed satisfied. "Where, exactly, are your friends?"

"In the West Country," invented Aurora. "Not far from Bath." It was the first place she thought of. Her mother had recently begun to voice her wish to visit the city of Bath, where she hoped the spa water might relieve her swollen seamstress's finger joints.

"I know your parents are both deceased, but do you have other relatives?" enquired Joe.

"No," said Aurora quickly. "My father was considerably older than my mother, and the last of his family living. My mother's parents have also passed on, and although she had a sister, we have never had anything to do with her. I do not believe my aunt ever married. I do not even know if she lives still."

She was pleased with this fabrication, which had come to her instantly. At a stroke, grandparents, aunts, uncles and cousins had been obliterated.

Joe pondered her answers. "Then soon, you will be utterly alone in the world."

"That is so."

"What will you do, when your brother ... when you are finally alone?" he asked.

"I have not decided," seemed the safest reply. "I may go back to Bath."

"And face your brother's creditors?"

She shrugged. "I must bear whatever comes to me, I suppose."

"The Lord will provide," agreed Joe. He shifted on the bench a little. His expression had become earnest. "Speaking of the Lord ... my sister tells me you have been brought up in the Protestant faith."

Aurora could guess why he was questioning her so carefully. From Miss Drayton's point of view, marriage to Joe Deede would be far, far preferable to being left to make her own way in the world. Because she had no family to object, she could take the irrevocable step of converting to Catholicism in order to become his wife, as his father had done in order to marry Joe's mother.

Aurora began to despise herself for continuing this charade. To mislead a man in such an important matter as love and marriage, to lie before God like the worst sinner ever consigned to damnation, was despicable. She wished she really *were* lonely Miss Drayton, who cared so little for her religion that she might be persuaded to abandon it for a rich husband. As it was, she found herself wilfully deceiving a man innocent of everything but falling in love with her.

"Yes, sir, that is true," she told him. "But I have never been very strict in my religion. My brother is more so."

He caught the sorrow in her voice, though he could not know its real cause. "Does speaking of such things cause you pain?"

"Forgive me, sir," she said, bowing her head. "I am merely distressed by the thought that before I can make any plans about where to go or anything else, my dear brother must be buried, and in a Protestant churchyard."

He nodded towards her wine glass, which she had set beside her on the bench. "Then drink, and let us walk a little while, before we meet the others for supper. The exercise will give us an appetite."

Aurora was relieved to end the conversation. When she had finished her wine she took Joe's arm and they set off along a different alley from the one they had taken before. It emerged into the main concourse, where the crowd had increased. "How will all these people be fed?" asked Aurora in wonder.

"It is managed somehow," Joe assured her. "And you must understand that not every visitor will have the means to purchase a supper ticket."

"Oh! I hope this entertainment is not proving very expensive for you!"

"Not at all. It is a very great pleasure to provide you with an enjoyable evening," he said stiffly.

Aurora was again assailed by guilt. She squeezed his arm. "You are a good man, Joe Deede," she said warmly. "You are altogether a better person than Aurora Drayton!"

He began to respond with a pleasantry. But suddenly he stopped, transfixed by something ahead. Aurora found her hand clasped more tightly to his side. "Good God!" he exclaimed in an outraged whisper. "The effrontery of that man!"

Aurora followed his gaze. Her heart jumped so violently she had to put her hand on her breast. Not three yards away, walking towards them with the rest of the throng, were Edward and Richard. They appeared as they had when she had first seen them in St James's Park: two young gentlemen, finely dressed, extravagantly bewigged, wearing their swords with a confident air.

Her cheeks had instantly reddened, and she put up her fan. She must not betray she had ever seen either of these men before. Her brain raced as she tried to piece together the events of the evening. Edward had left their lodgings while she was still dressing, reminding her he was going to meet Richard at Will's Coffee House. He had not been wearing this finery then, so he must have returned to change after she had gone to Mill Street. What mischief was he up to?

"I know not who the taller man is," said Joe, "but the shorter one is the son of my father's greatest enemy, now deceased, I am glad to say. The son is as great a villain as his father was, and as great an enemy of our family."

Aurora tried to recover her wits, and remember to be Miss Drayton. "But, Joe," she said as mildly as she could, "we are in a public place. It must be merely by chance that your path has crossed this man's tonight."

"That is so. You are quite right." He patted her hand again. His voice was calmer, but his chest rose and fell rapidly. The sight of Edward had greatly unsettled him. "We shall ignore them."

But as Aurora might have predicted, Edward was not of the same mind. He approached boldly and removed his hat. "Mr Deede, in*deed*!" he cried, with an exaggerated bow. Richard, grinning, bowed equally low. Aurora could not fathom this nonsense.

"Good evening, Mr Francis." Joe did not bow, but regarded both gentlemen with suspicion.

"Allow me to introduce my friend, Mr Augustus Hoggart," said Edward, indicating Richard. "Augustus, this is Mr Josiah Deede, of Mill Street, Mayfair."

"Odd!" exclaimed Richard foppishly, his fingers cupping his chin. "I would have thought Mr Josiah Deede, the esteemed attorney, to be rather *older*."

"This is the esteemed attorney's son," Edward told him. His eyes then travelled back to Joe, who was still regarding him and Richard coldly. "Mr Deede, may Augustus and I have the pleasure of being introduced to your fair companion?"

Joe gave an impatient sigh. He could not, for courtesy's sake, refuse. "Gentlemen, this is Miss Aurora Drayton, of Covent Garden." His grip on Aurora's arm did not relent. "Miss Drayton and I are on our way to meet the rest of our party for supper, and must take our leave. Fare you well. Come, Aurora."

Before she had time to make a curtsey, Joe tried to pull her away. But at that moment Mrs Fellowes and Mrs Partridge appeared. Pushing herself eagerly between their shoulders was Celia, whose face, already pink from excitement and the heat of the evening, turned pinker when she saw the two strangers. "Oh, Joe!" she cried. "You have met someone you know! Do introduce us!"

Again, courtesy would not allow Joe to refuse. "My sister, Miss Celia Deede, and our friends Mrs Fellowes and Mrs Partridge," he announced, without looking at the two men. "Ladies, this gentleman is Mr Hoggart, and this is Mr Francis."

Celia's expression changed. "Mr *Edward* Francis?"

"The very same," replied Joe bitterly. "I would have walked past him if he had not insisted otherwise. But come, Celia, we must to supper. My dear Mrs Fellowes, Mrs Partridge, will you join us?"

This time he succeeded in moving the party of ladies on. Edward and Richard glanced at each other and began to walk towards the supper tables too. Joe ignored them, but Celia could not contain her delight at falling into the company of the famous Edward Francis, whom her father and brother had spoken of with such contempt, and whose fortune had landed so spectacularly in her own lap.

"What are you doing here, Mr Francis?" she asked him pertly. "I am surprised you can afford the price of admission! Or did your friend pay for you?"

"Celia!" admonished Joe. "Do not debase yourself in speaking so." He turned to the two older ladies with apology. "Mr Francis's family has long been at enmity with ours, and Celia has not encountered him before. Though I have." He looked sidelong at Edward. "However, I confess myself bewildered as to why he has decided to adhere to our party."

"I am grieved to hear that," said Edward. "I would have thought my motive would be obvious. You are in the company of four charming ladies, and Augustus and I are in the company of none. Will you not share them with us for a little while?"

Mrs Fellowes succumbed immediately to this flattery. "Why, Mr Francis, I believe you are flirting with us!" she trilled. "But you would be far better to flirt with Celia and Aurora, you know – Mrs Partridge and I are spoken for!"

"Quite so, madam," agreed Edward, bowing. He took

a step nearer Aurora. "Miss Drayton, you must be at a loss to understand the cause of Miss Deede's animosity. I confess I am too. Now that I have seen her for the first time, I consider her a very pretty, amiable young lady. As, no doubt, her brother considers *you*."

"Enough, sir!" Joe could no longer keep his countenance. "I insist that you remove yourself from our company. We have not invited you to join us for supper—"

"More's the pity!" put in Richard. "I like nothing better than supping in the company of ladies!"

"And we *will not* invite you," continued Joe with contempt. "You, sir," he said to Richard, "are as conceited a puppy as your companion. I will not allow either of you to make free with my sister, Miss Drayton or our friends. I bid you both farewell."

Compressing his lips, he strode on, followed by Celia and the others. But Aurora had freed her hand from Joe's grasp. She fell into step with Edward and Richard, a few yards behind the others, avoiding Joe's sight by mingling with the increasingly dense crowd. "Are you *completely* deranged?" she hissed at Edward.

"No, I am merely bored with Samuel Marshall's company."

She could not show her anger in her face in such a public place, but she thrust it into her voice. "You came to spy on me, did you not? You do not trust me. Admit it!"

"We came to protect you," said Edward calmly. "My distrust of Joe Deede grows daily. I am afraid I cannot find him as innocent as you profess him to be."

Aurora's indignation did not abate. "Your arrogance..." She stopped, and glanced coldly at Richard.

"The arrogance of you *both* is breathtaking. Will you risk destroying everything I have tried to do, in order to spy on your own spy?"

Edward drew breath, but she was too incensed to let him speak.

"Why involve Richard?" she asked. "Oh, I *know* why! You thought two pairs of eyes would be better than one, did you not, in case you missed a coquettish glance, or some lover's sign I might have given Joe Deede?"

Edward's eyes glittered, but he kept his countenance. Taking her elbow, he drew her into an alley so rich with blossom they were immediately invisible to passers-by. "It was necessary to bring Richard, whom Joe Deede has never seen and whose identity he does not know," he told her firmly. "Being in the company of a droll young fellow, a part I think you will agree Richard plays very well, made my running into your party more plausible than if I had appeared alone."

"But why did you have to appear at all?" demanded Aurora.

"I had to satisfy myself that my suspicions of Joe Deede are well founded. My appearance clearly disturbed him, did you not see? He is no more at peace with his father's sudden inheritance than I am, though he pretends otherwise. He is as suspicious of me as I am of him. I will wager he knows about the key. He may well know about the letter too. He is waiting to act. You are in danger of discovery, and more."

Aurora barely listened. "Edward, hear this," she commanded coldly: "I refuse to continue in this enterprise if you will not trust me to accomplish my task alone. You said I have the attributes of a good spy, did you not? So I would thank you to allow me to discharge my duties. Now, Joe will be seeking me. I must return to my party."

He did not release his grip on her elbow. Aurora turned to see Richard guarding the entrance to the alley. She turned back to Edward. "I insist, sir, that you let me be!"

She watched the purposefulness of his expression disappear, and resignation take its place. "Very well," he said, letting go of her arm. As he contemplated her his eyes filled with a soft light. "But do me the honour of remembering, in your dealings with the Deede family, that it is *I* – not Joe Deede – who loves you truly. If disaster should befall you, my remorse would last past death."

Aurora gave him a final indignant look, then brushed past Richard and stepped out of the alley. Joe was scanning the crowd with a pained, restless expression. "I am here, Joe," she reassured him. "I was detained by people getting in my way."

"Did those two men speak to you again?"

"Of course not," soothed Aurora. "They are gone. Let us enjoy our supper in peace."

A Lace-Edged Glove

Aurora awoke the next day feeling hot. Brilliant sunlight imprinted a small square on the grimy floorboards of her room. It was Sunday; a church bell tolled for nine o'clock service. Despite her good supper at Spring Gardens, she wanted her breakfast, and it was time Edward woke up anyway. She got up and opened her chamber door. The outer room was empty, the bed still made. Edward had not returned.

She crossed the room, unlocked the door and stood on the landing, listening. Mary was going about her morning chores. Aurora heard the *clump, clump* of her heavy shoes, and the *click, click* of Mr Marshall's stick as he made his way downstairs. She lifted the breakfast tray Mary had left outside the door and placed it on the table. Then she closed the door and turned the key.

The coffee was long cold, but she drank greedily. She cut a thick slice of bread and butter, and took it into her room, wondering why Edward had not come back. Had he stayed at the Black Swan with Richard? Or had they both gone to Hartford House? Why, after what he had said about keeping the door locked, had he left her alone all night?

She finished the slice of bread and licked butter off her fingers, thinking about Joe. She knew quite well why Edward was convinced of his duplicity: he was jealous of the attentions Joe was paying her. Aurora was *not* convinced, but in the short time she had known Edward Francis she had learned to respect his wisdom. Would he have embarked upon last night's reckless adventure without good cause? If he was sure that Joe knew more than he betrayed, should she be so sure he did not?

She tried to master her unease. She knew she should trust her husband; without trust she was lost. And she hoped he would trust her, as he had agreed to last night under the blossom trees. But her imagination framed the memory of Joe's handsome countenance, and the amiable attentiveness he had shown her. He had not chosen to fall in love with a Protestant woman, but now that he had, he was making the best of it. His quizzing her about her lack of family connections and uncertain future had a very important purpose. And since it was not Aurora *Francis* he held in his heart, but Aurora *Drayton*, what harm was he doing anyone but himself?

She sat on the bed a little longer, thinking hard. Then she went to her trunk and pulled out a grey cotton dress, sprigged with blue and trimmed with white. It was light material, but the weather was warm enough for it. She shook it out and held it against herself. The glass told her that yes, the dress suited her well; the bodice was low but not too revealing, and the pattern reflected the blue of her eyes. With white ribbons on her straw hat, she would be fit to charm Joe Deede. Or, for that matter, whomever else came in her way.

She was searching for her summer petticoat when she heard Edward's key turn in the lock.

"Aurora! Are you awake?" There was more than urgency in his voice.

Aurora rose and opened her bedroom door. Framed by the side curls of his wig, Edward's face was shadowed by anxiety. He was still dressed in last night's finery, but his shirt had been pulled awry at the neck, and his breeches were muddied. Aurora stiffened. "What has happened?"

He ignored her question, preoccupied with others. "Was the key still in the lock of the writing desk? Did you retrieve it?"

"Yes, on both accounts."

"And where is it now?"

"It is with the letter, at the bottom of this trunk."

His eyes fell on the open trunk, and the dress laid out on the bed. He held out his hand. "Give me them both, the key and the letter."

"But surely *I* must keep them," reasoned Aurora, "since I must restore the letter to its hiding place as soon as possible?"

"There is no need of that now. Give me them."

Puzzled, but not daring to press him further, she knelt and rummaged for the letter and the key. When she handed them to him, he put them in the deepest pocket of his coat. "Richard is in an upstairs room at the inn, under the name of Mr Augustus Hoggart. I am afraid that our situation has become more dangerous."

"Since your reckless behaviour last night?"

"I am never reckless. But we are discovered."

Aurora froze. "How?"

Edward pushed the sprigged gown aside and sat on her bed. Still kneeling by the trunk, she watched while he removed his wig and rubbed his scalp. He was exhausted.

"Richard and I stayed within Spring Gardens until your party departed for the ferry," he began in a low voice, "then we caught the next one. I wished to protect you as long as I could."

Aurora bridled at this, though she made no protest aloud.

"We walked together as far as the piazza, here in Covent Garden," continued Edward. "Then we parted, Richard for the Black Swan, I for these lodgings. But before I had gone ten yards I heard a scuffle and a scream, and ran back. Richard lay upon the cobbles. He had been struck on the head."

"Who would do such a thing?" gasped Aurora incredulously, her brain immediately busy with questions. "Did they mistake him for you? Were they trying to kill him?"

Edward gave a sigh. "They did not mistake him, neither did they mean to leave him for dead. I am convinced they intended to render him unconscious, and for me to find him. They must have followed us, seen us part, and pounced while I was still close enough to hear Richard's cry. It was staged, without doubt."

"But to what end?"

"They left this in Richard's waistcoat pocket. Here, read it."

Aurora took the piece of paper he offered. In a haphazard style, probably disguised, were written the words, *I know who you are.*

"Do you understand the import of this?" asked Edward.

"Your identity is discovered," she replied, raising her eyes to his face, "by someone who would harm you. Beyond that I have no explanation."

He nodded. "Do you see anything else on the page?"

She looked again. In the corner of the paper was a scribble she could not make out. "What does it say here?" she asked, pointing.

Edward's voice was still soft, but steady, and full of implication. "It is a crude representation of the family crest of the Deedes."

Aurora met his eyes. "So … the person or persons who attacked you did so on behalf of Josiah Deede?"

"Aye," said Edward with sorrow. "It seems his hatred of me is unabated, despite his successful theft of my inheritance."

Silence fell between them. Aurora held out the paper; she wanted rid of it, and Edward took it, recognizing her revulsion. "Someone must have been following us," he said. "How much Josiah Deede knows – whether 'Miss Drayton' has been discovered too – we can only conjecture."

"And he wanted…" Aurora's throat had contracted. She could barely speak. "He wanted to give you a warning. A threat."

Edward nodded wearily. "We are all in danger."

Aurora knelt there on the floor, her hands in her lap, her heartbeat unsteady. The return of the letter was now no longer necessary, as Edward had said. Josiah Deede had found the key, and discovered the theft. Afraid that Edward knew the secret, and would continue the blackmail, he had resorted to paying ruffians to follow Edward, attack

Richard and leave the threatening note. In huntsman's terms, he was trying to flush Edward out and force him into the path of danger. If Edward showed himself, Deede would be waiting.

She swallowed. Tears had crept into her eyes, though she did not know why. Did she weep for Edward, disinherited, defeated, and now threatened, seeking a fruitless revenge on a powerful man with ruthless associates? Or for Joe, whose father's conduct had now ensured that his courtship of the amiable Miss Drayton was irredeemably, irretrievably over?

"I must go to Richard," said Edward, rousing himself. He put on his wig and stood up. "I came only to collect the key and the letter, which we cannot leave hidden in this room, and to warn you to lock the door and admit no one."

Aurora rose too, so shakily that she had to place her hand on the open lid of the trunk. "When will you return?"

"When I can leave him," said Edward. He looked at her intently. "Fare thee well, my dear Aurora."

He walked to the outer door and she followed him, intending to lock it after he had gone. But then he stopped unexpectedly and whirled round, his hand going to his coat pocket. "I almost forgot this!"

He handed her a letter. It was addressed to Hartford House in familiar handwriting and sealed with a familiar seal. "Richard brought it, but I have not had the opportunity to give it to you until now," said Edward.

And before she realized he had done it, he had kissed her brow and quitted the room.

*   *   *

Dacre Street, Westminster
May 3rd, 1700

My dearest, dearest Aurora,

    Mrs Edward Francis! Have you been practising your new signature? Hester says if I finish this note before eight o'clock she will take it to the Bell, and put it in the coach that passes through Islington. Please send one of your servants to do the same with your reply, or if Mr Allcott should be in town he is always welcome to deliver a letter in person.

    I miss you already, my dear sister, though you were married but four days ago. That night, we were so late home from Hartford House, and the bedchamber was so lonely without you, that Eleanora came and slept in your place. I confess we wept, but only tears of happiness. I have many questions about what happened to you that night, but I will not ask any of them, of course.

    Please, please write and tell me you are in good health and happy. I await your reply with great impatience. And now Hester is waiting, so I must break off.

    With fondest love, and the same from Eleanora,
      Flora Mary Eversedge

That evening, in the dancing room, Aurora held her sister's letter close to the candle and read it for the fourth time. It interested Aurora to think that it was now five days since Flora had sat down at the little writing desk in the drawing room and taken up her pen. During that period, the letter had gone by coach to Islington, where it had been picked up by Richard's servant and taken to Hartford House. Richard had brought it with him to London when he arrived yesterday. She added the days together – four days between the wedding and the writing of the letter and five days for it to get to her. Was her marriage truly only *nine days* old? It seemed astonishing that everything she had believed before it took place had vanished, as instantly and irrevocably as any of Flora's more far-fetched fancies.

Edward had still not returned. She had locked the door as he had instructed, and had spent a lonely and fearful day. She was now sitting cross-legged on her bed in her nightdress, every muscle in her body tense, unable to sleep until she heard his familiar footsteps.

She guessed it must be near to eleven o'clock at night. She could hear the servants moving around, and there was still traffic in the street. She put down Flora's letter and was about to snuff the candle when she heard a sound that was not Mary shutting up the house. She tiptoed to the outer door and listened. Below, the sounds of booted footsteps, a raised masculine voice and the grumble of Mary's remonstrations got louder as the footsteps mounted the stairs.

She tried not to panic. It must be someone known to Mr Marshall. But the door handle rattled, then a deafening knocking began. "I demand that you open this door!" The voice belonged to Joe Deede.

Aurora's heart thudded. Joe was still knocking on the door. When she did not answer, he began to kick it. It creaked and strained under his assault. It was an old door with an ordinary iron latch and lock. If Aurora did not open it, it would soon succumb.

She heard an inarticulate shout and the sound of scuffling feet. She backed away from the door just before it banged against the wall and Joe crashed into the room. He staggered against the table, uttered an oath, grasped the back of a chair and regarded Aurora furiously. His breath came hoarsely. "So this is how *Miss Drayton* repays our hospitality, is it?"

Aurora's body tingled with shock. She hardly recognized Joe's features, distorted as they were with indignation and rage. His face was flushed with exertion, his eyes pink-rimmed. But she tried to preserve her wits and think. It was no use trying to keep up her pretence; Miss Drayton's consumptive brother who never went out was clearly absent. But it would not do to confess everything either, at least until she was certain how much Joe knew, and how he had found it out.

She kept her expression passive, though beneath her nightgown her heart was galloping. "And is this," she asked calmly, "how a gentleman pays a call on a lady, breaking down her door in the middle of the night, when she is not dressed?" She had left the inner door open and began to make her way towards her room. "I beg you, give me leave to make myself presentable."

"Do not walk away from me!" he roared.

Aurora stopped, but she regarded him with disdain and gestured to a chair. "Please sit down."

"I will not sit down," he said petulantly. "I insist that you tell me who you really are, and what your business is with Edward Francis!"

Fear gripped her. Edward's suspicions had been well founded. After she had left Mill Street on Friday, Joe must have found the skeleton key in the lock of the cabinet, wondered what it was and alerted his father. Discovering that the letter was gone, Josiah must have left the key there to trap her, knowing she would remove it when she returned to the house on Saturday evening. As, of course, she did. Evidently, Josiah had told his son she was an impostor. But had he told Joe about the contents of the letter?

"I am Aurora Drayton," she said blankly, "as well you know."

He crossed the room swiftly and seized her left arm. "Do not deny that you live here with Edward Francis! Edward Drayton does not exist, and whoever you are, you are not Aurora Drayton!"

Aurora's mind raced. Josiah's henchmen must have been following her since the discovery of the key. Edward and Richard's late departure from Spring Gardens made it easy for the villains to follow them, attack Richard and leave the threatening note. Earlier, Josiah's men had seen her return to the lodgings alone, and this morning they had watched Edward leave for the Black Swan, and not yet return.

Evidently, if they had reported this to Josiah, he had then reported it to his son. Joe Deede had chosen very carefully the moment to make his assault.

He shook her arm, his grip tightening. "If you will not confess it, then be in no doubt that I will beat it out of you!"

A boorish bully, accustomed to violence. So Henry Francis had been correct about Joe Deede after all.

"I am not afraid of you," she told him. She tried to keep her voice steady, but a constriction in her chest prevented her from drawing sufficient breath. The house was silent. She wondered whether Mary had gone to tell Mr Marshall of the angry young visitor. With his gouty foot, Mr Marshall could not climb the attic stairs, and William would be long gone at this hour.

"Indeed? Alas, you should be!" His face, a mask of

frustration, was very close to Aurora's. His breath smelled sourly of gin. "And you *will* tell me what his intention is, if you wish to preserve your beauty."

This was such a cowardly threat that Aurora's fear became scorn. "Only a man who is not a man will threaten a woman," she said coldly. "I pray you, leave me be."

His eyes hardened, and he began to twist her arm. Pain shot through her elbow. She gasped, but locked her jaw, refusing to scream. Her teeth ground against one another as he pushed her arm behind her back and applied such pressure to it she thought it must burst from its socket. All the while, he demanded that she tell him what Edward Francis had instructed her to do. "He wants to ruin my father, does he not? He thinks my father has stolen his inheritance." He twisted her arm higher. "Though he has not, has he? Tell me you know he has not!"

Aurora's determination not to show her pain was making her faint. Silver motes floated before her eyes. But her arm felt on the point of breaking, and to her shame, she blurted, "He has not!"

The pressure on her arm did not diminish. "Henry Francis was a blackmailer, was he not? Say it!"

"Henry Francis was…"

She could speak no more. Unconsciously, she had begun to cry. It was not the sustained weeping she remembered from her father's funeral, or the girlish tears a quarrel with Flora would produce. It was an anguished, shuddering, sobbing onslaught that soaked her face and burned her lungs. "Please, please…" came out in a whisper. She had no breath. She closed her eyes.

And then she heard a voice that was not Joe Deede's.

"Leave hold of her, or I will have your head off!"

Her tormentor loosened, but did not relinquish, his grip. Aurora blinked frantically, trying to clear her vision. Edward stood in the doorway, his sword drawn, his eyes like gemstones in the pale mask of his face.

"Leave her be, I say, and conduct yourself like a man!" he taunted.

Aurora found herself released. She sank to the floor. Her tears were subsiding, but she was not yet mistress of herself, and trembled as if possessed by a fever.

Joe had not drawn his own sword, but when he spoke to Edward his voice was hostile and impatient. "Miss Drayton, as she calls herself, is a thief."

Aurora's eyes were closed, but she heard the squeak of a loose floorboard as Edward crossed the room to kneel beside her. She felt the touch of his hand upon her cheek. "Where are you hurt?" he asked.

"My arm, my shoulder." She opened her eyes. Though her sight was tear-washed, she could see the depth of Edward's rage. His face was pinched, and whiter than plaster.

He stood up and re-sheathed his sword. "I insist you leave my chambers immediately," he told Joe Deede. "This lady must be attended to."

"This *lady*, if that is what she is" – Aurora heard the thump of Joe's fist on the table – "has been employed for a sizeable fee, I presume – to pose as your sister. Her instructions, no doubt, were to make the acquaintance of my family, and, acting as your spy, accuse my father of wrongdoing. You could not be satisfied with the judge's verdict on the contesting of your father's will, could you? Well, sir, your clever little accomplice lost no time in finding proof, but, alas, not the proof you expected. Her theft of a letter in my father's possession has shown that Henry Francis was a blackmailer!"

"Do not say that, sir…"

Joe ignored Edward's interruption. "Your father changed his will to repay my father because he feared God's punishment. You see? Your fortune was made by illegal means – I will not scruple to say again, by *blackmail*. And now, by God's will, it is back in the right hands." He laughed humourlessly. "I see by the squalor of this room that you are already becoming used to doing without it!"

There was silence. Aurora wondered what Edward could do to protect her, or himself. Joe Deede seemed to have outwitted them.

"Very well, I deny it no longer." Edward did not sound outwitted. He said the words stoutly, as a statement of fact. "My wife showed me the letter, and—"

Colour flooded Joe's cheeks. "Your *wife*!"

"And I told her of my father's grave affliction, as I will now tell you," continued Edward. "For the last ten years of his life, my father was so crippled with rheumatism that he had to use an amanuensis."

Joe made a sound like "Hrrmph!" He looked at Edward with contempt. "Such as you yourself?"

Edward did not fall into the trap. "I am aware that anyone, myself included, could have written that letter," he told Joe frostily. "But if I were privy to whatever it is that your father will pay to keep secret, why have I not continued to blackmail him when my father died five months ago?"

Joe did not reply.

"Furthermore," said Edward, "you persist in believing that my father altered his will because he was overcome with remorse about blackmailing your father. You say that he must have dictated that blackmail letter, and heaven knows how many others, to another person. Well, let me give you another version of the story. My father *did* know your father's secret, but he took it with him to the grave, never considering using it to his advantage, though it was in his power to do so. Your father was tricked by the unspeakable villainy of the writer of those letters, and Henry Francis was never the blackmailer at all!"

Joe struck a frustrated blow to the mantelpiece, near where he stood. He could not refute the logic of Edward's conclusion. "Henry Francis was a poor apology for a man!" he bellowed. Another blow. "A coward!" Another blow. "A man who made an enemy out of a friend, then stole his money! He was not a man, but a monstrous, godless beast!"

"Then what is *your* father?" Edward had been driven too far. "A man who murders his former friend in order to forge his will? It is not *my* father that is the godless beast, but yours!"

All the colour had gone from Joe Deede's face. "Do you dare to accuse my father of *murder*?" he asked incredulously.

"Indeed I do. And of forgery and gross deception." Edward's words were followed by the sound of metal on metal. Aurora scrambled painfully to her feet. Swaying, she gripped the edge of the table. Edward had drawn his sword and was holding it upright before him, its blade six inches from his face. "I will fight to the death for my father's honour," he said stoutly.

Joe drew his own sword and, like Edward, held it

upright "And so will I, for *my* father's honour."

Grimacing at the pain in her left arm, Aurora lunged with her other arm for Edward's sword hand, like an anxious mother trying to remove a sharp stick from her son. "No! No!" she implored. "I beg you, do not do this. He will kill you. Please, do not allow him to incense you!"

"Peace!" Edward's eyes had lost their glitter. They looked at her grimly. "I will deal with this."

"No, Edward, I cannot stand aside and watch you place yourself in death's way," persisted Aurora. "This man is a swordsman, in constant practice. It is an unfair match."

"Indeed it is," said Joe Deede, tilting his chin. "Sir, you know not what awaits you."

"It is a question of honour," Edward told Aurora. "I cannot allow my father to stand accused of blackmail without demanding satisfaction on the matter."

Aurora knew this. She also understood that Joe must defend his own father's honour, and accept the challenge. She released Edward's wrist and looked at Joe. Only last night she had wished she were truly Miss Drayton, free and ready to marry a man to whom she was attracted, and who was attracted to her. Now, as she looked at him standing before Edward in the mean little room, his raised sword glinting in the moonlight, his face full of the certainty of victory, she knew Joe Deede had duped her far more successfully than she had duped him.

"Very well," she said bitterly. "Do your worst, the both of you."

On the table lay her gloves, where she had discarded them when she came in. They were her new ones, made of kid leather edged with lace. Edward picked up the right-hand glove and threw it on the floor at Joe Deede's feet. "I challenge you to defend the honour and reputation of your family."

Joe stooped and picked up the glove. Aurora stared at it, invested as it was with an importance beyond its appearance, wondering if somehow its femininity could make void the masculine vow it represented. The desire to scream with horror constricted her throat.

"I accept the challenge," said Joe. He dropped the glove, returned his sword to its sheath and bowed. "At dawn, sir, the day after tomorrow, upon Lincoln's Inn Fields."

Edward bowed too, and Joe strode from the room. Only when the sound of his footsteps had gone, and the street door had slammed, did Edward put down his own sword. "Remind me tomorrow," he said, looking ruefully at Aurora, "to get this old thing sharpened."

Aurora's legs would no longer support her. She sat down on Edward's bed. The room swung around her. "Edward," she said, her voice sounding far away, as if it were someone else's voice heard through a wall. "Edward, my husband, I beg you, do not do this."

He removed his sword-belt and his wig, put them on the table and took off his coat. Not having yet been able to change his clothes, it was his best coat, the dark red one with gold-trimmed buttonholes. Under it he was still wearing the dishevelled shirt he had donned for Spring Gardens, his embroidered waistcoat and his dirtied breeches. He set the jacket on the back of the chair, rumpled his hair with the palm of his hand, and sighed deeply.

Aurora knew that all the time he was doing this he was thinking. It was becoming clear that he was much, much better at thinking than she was. Tears stung her eyes. "I am so sorry," she said in a whisper. "I should have been more vigilant. I forgot the key. I have proved worse than useless to you; I have led you into mortal danger." Her cheeks were wet with tears, but she made no attempt to wipe them away. "You must withdraw from the duel. Please, please…"

Gently, he took her hands in his. "I cannot withdraw. It is a question of honour. "

"But you are not a match for Joe Deede!" she protested. "You do not follow sporting pursuits. You do not ride or hawk. You like books and music, and carry a sword only because it is part of every gentleman's attire, like his wig or his waistcoat. Surely there is a less violent way to settle this dispute?"

Edward wiped her cheeks with his thumbs. "Are you suggesting that I arm myself with a treatise on natural history, and Deede defend himself with a violin?"

"How can you *joke*?" Aurora was aghast. "He will kill you!"

"Then I will die defending my father's honour. There are worse ways to end one's life."

"Edward!" An agitation she had never felt before rushed over her. She gripped his wrist with her good hand. "You cannot throw your life away in this stubborn way. I cannot bear it. Have you forgotten that *I am your wife*?"

He regarded her for a long moment. Then he removed her hand from his wrist and drew it to his breast. "No, I have not forgotten. You are my wife and I am your husband, much to Joe Deede's chagrin. But you married me believing I was about to die, and that you would soon be a widow. A rich one, but a widow nevertheless. If I am killed by a blade rather than an illness, you will still be my widow, only you will not be rich. The Deedes do not know who you were before you were Edward Francis's secret wife. You may return to your family and forget all about me."

"How can I do that?" she protested. "If you are killed, I will not rest until I have had my revenge. I will pursue Josiah Deede relentlessly. Richard will help me. Your family honour, and your fortune, will be restored."

He smiled sadly. "Think of your mother, and your beloved sisters…"

"It *is* because of them that I must do this! If you are killed, the stolen fortune is mine in law, and I will do everything I can to retrieve my rightful property so that I can give my mother the material comfort she deserves and help my sisters to find suitable husbands."

He regarded her, his lips compressed, the skin under his eyes wrinkling with the intensity of his stare. Aurora did not flinch.

"Then do as you wish," he said, and bent his head to kiss her hand.

She did not know what to say. She could not explain the force of her feelings, or how sudden and strong was her desire that he should live and continue to be her husband. The seriousness of his situation, and the tenderness of his action, made all the words she knew seem redundant. She gazed helplessly at him as he raised his head.

"Tomorrow may be my last day on earth," he said. "If I do not return from Lincoln's Inn on Tuesday morning, you must—"

She put up her right hand to stop him. "But you *will* return, Edward! God will surely protect you!"

Murder Begets Murder

The next morning Aurora found herself again alone in the attic rooms. Edward's dark red suit lay folded upon the chest in which his clothes were kept, and his long wig was on its stand. He had dressed plainly for whatever business he was about today. The outer door, its lock broken, hung half open.

It took her a long time to dress in her sprigged gown. Her shoulder throbbed with insistent pain. She managed to wash her face, but she could not pin up her hair with one hand, so she left it as she had worn it for sleep, in a single plait. She sat at the table, read the precious letter from Flora two more times, then folded it and put it in her pocket.

It was after two o'clock when Mary came to clear the breakfast dishes. She gave Aurora an inquisitive look. Aurora knew it was foolish to pretend nothing had happened. Mary might be graceless and taciturn, but she was not an imbecile.

"I thank you, Mary, for your attempts to dissuade my visitor from coming upstairs last night," she said. "But he was incensed, and would not listen to reason."

Mary bobbed a curtsey. "Yes, 'm."

"Mr Drayton dealt with him. He will not come back."

"Yes, 'm." Mary stretched for the butter dish, which was at Aurora's elbow. Aurora, who was expected to help Hester at home, unthinkingly reached for it too. She gasped, the jolt of pain bringing tears to her eyes. "You 'urt, Miss?" asked Mary.

"It is nothing. Um … Mr Drayton will speak to Mr Marshall about the door lock. He will of course pay for its repair."

Another curtsey, then Mary picked up the loaded tray, still eyeing Aurora. "Very well, 'm."

Mary elbowed the half-open door wider and bustled through with her tray. Aurora heard her footsteps on the stairs, William's inept whistling and the squawking of the chickens in the yard behind the house. Then the street door banged and Edward's boots sounded on every second stair as he ran up to the attic rooms. Normal sounds in a normal world.

But Aurora's world was no longer normal. When Edward came in, put a grease-stained package from a pie shop on the table and sat down in the other chair, she knew she had never felt such dread. She looked at him intently, imprinting his every feature on her memory.

"Your shoulder hurts you, does it not?" he asked.

She nodded. "But not as sorely as my dread of Joe Deede."

"Do not think about him. You are nervous because you are in pain." From the pocket of his waistcoat he took a small bottle. "I have brought you a draught of laudanum. It will make you sleep. You will not be anxious, and when you wake up your arm will feel better, and all will be over."

"I thank you, but I cannot sleep," she told him gravely. Unbidden by any conscious instruction, her good hand grasped his forearm as it lay on the table. Touching him, feeling his living flesh through his shirt and coat sleeve, seemed compellingly important. The idea that after tomorrow that flesh might be for ever cold seemed ludicrous, the suggestion of a madman. "I wish to be with you every minute until dawn."

His eyes shone as he put the bottle containing the sleeping draught on the table and took her hand in both his. He seemed to wish to smile, but kept his countenance as grave as her own. "Be in no doubt of my gratitude for your concern, my dear," he said, "but that cannot be. I have been to a knife-grinder this morning and had him sharpen my sword, and now I must rouse Richard."

Aurora's heart thudded, but she recovered herself enough to voice her surprise. "Surely Richard should rest today?"

"He has rested long enough. He has duties," said Edward briskly. "He must act as my second."

Aurora pictured Richard's thin, watchful face and his bandaged head. She could not imagine him performing the duties of the duellist's second man, making sure the rules of duelling were followed, calling the *en garde* for the start of the fight, dealing with his wounded, or dead, friend after the event. "I cannot think he is well enough for such a task," she said dubiously.

The sounds of doors opening and closing and of Samuel Marshall's voice came from below. Edward spoke softly. "He will have to be. He is a good swordsman, and even though he is injured I need his help. I must practise for many hours today. It is a while since I drew my sword." He smiled thinly. "Until last night, that is."

Aurora was dismayed. Women could not enter fencing-halls. "But I cannot stay here alone, Edward, waiting for you. I shall go mad."

"Then take the laudanum and sleep. I will not be back tonight. Richard and I intend to go straight to Lincoln's Inn Fields from the fencing-hall."

Aurora gazed at him blankly. "But the duel is not until dawn!"

"The sun does not rise until half past five," he explained gently, "but there are too many people going about their business by then. Deede will be there before four o'clock, you may be sure."

Aurora's heart felt swollen, as if it were too small to hold the many things she wanted to tell him. She wished he knew that his death would break her heart, and that she would give herself to another man only from the strictest necessity, as she had promised, that day in the drawing-room, to give herself to Edward. He had stirred something in her beyond the compassion, pity or indignation aroused by his plight – something inexpressible, yet which she longed to express. And although he seemed aware of the shift her feelings had undergone, he gave her no opportunity to speak of it. Wiser than she was, he would not allow her to say or do anything she might afterwards regret, at least until the outcome of tomorrow's meeting on Lincoln's Inn Fields was known.

So she said nothing of these thoughts. She put her hands in her lap and summoned a meek expression. "Very well,

I shall obey. I shall sit here and write to my sister, and pray for your safe return."

"God will protect me, as you yourself believe," said Edward. "And I have right on my side."

Aurora nodded. Men always thought they had right on their side, whichever side they were on. "Beware, though," she warned, "and remember that it is your father's death that has led you to this. Murder, as is often said, begets murder."

Edward looked at her for a moment with his black eyes. Her heart quailed; she was near embracing him. But before she could move he stood and went to the door. "I bid you farewell," he said flatly, and departed, pulling the broken latch behind him.

Mary was sweeping the stairs. *Knock, knock, knock* went the brush against each riser. Aurora heard Edward exchange greetings with Mr Marshall. She looked at the package of food before her. Its smell nauseated her; she had no appetite. Wearily, she rose and went into her bedchamber, where she sat on the bed, nursing her arm and thinking.

Her shoulder felt red-hot, as if pierced by needles, but she did not take the laudanum Edward had brought. She stared at the wall and imagined the next day's events. Richard would come in the early hours and tell her Edward was dead. And she would tell Richard of her promise not to rest until she had exposed Josiah Deede and regained Henry Francis's fortune.

Tears threatened, but she quelled them. She must not sit here weeping. She was responsible now. Together she and Richard would mourn Edward, pretending to her mother and sisters that he had died suddenly of his illness. Richard would give her money, and she would continue to live in the city, never ceasing her pursuit of Josiah Deede. Only when Deede had been tried and hanged would she return to Dacre Street and tell her family the truth. She tried to imagine being a rich widow, spending Edward's fortune. But she could not; such a notion seemed fatuous. What did she care about the money if she were obliged to live her life alone?

Her heart leapt suddenly. She knew without question that she would lodge for ever above the bookshop and sew petticoats for bread if only Edward were alive, and by her side.

She got up and walked about the small room. Three steps this way, three steps that. And as she walked her desire to preserve Edward's life consumed her. She became more and more resolute. The duel must not take place.

Pain shot through her left shoulder as she pressed her fingers to her temples, trying to think. Where would Joe Deede be today, on a Monday afternoon? At home in Mill Street, taking tea with his sister? Was he at this very moment telling Celia that Aurora was an impostor, and that her husband had challenged him to a duel? A vision of Celia's horror-stricken face came into her mind, but she dismissed it. Celia had been a means to an end, and Aurora must suppress any guilt arising out of her treatment of her. A girl such as Celia would quickly find herself another "dearest friend".

She walked around the room again. At whatever cost to herself, her only choice was to persuade Joe Deede to withdraw his acceptance of the challenge. But she could not go to Mill Street as Miss Drayton, or as herself. She would have to become someone else. After all, she remained Edward's spy as well as his obedient wife. Aurora the obedient wife had told him she would stay in all day and pray for him. But Aurora the spy had no intention of giving him up to Joe Deede's sword without a fight of her own.

Her trunk still stood open by the bed. She took out the brown woollen gown she used to wear for helping her mother in the shop. Slowly, clenching her teeth whenever she had to use her left arm, she changed her clothes. She looped up her plait under her plainest cap and a small straw hat. Then she wrapped an old shawl she usually only wore indoors around her shoulders and tied it behind, servant-fashion. As an afterthought, she tucked her left arm inside it. The makeshift sling lessened the pain in her shoulder; she would be able to face with reasonable comfort whatever came to her today. She crossed the room to the mirror. To her satisfaction, it showed her a nondescript member of the servant class.

She set off towards Mayfair, a lively wind whisking her skirt. When she came within sight of the horse-trough, she noticed that an alley adjoining Conduit Street led past the back of the house. It was narrow and smelled foul, but widened into a yard where there were stables and a dairy. A woman in a pink second-hand gown, the skirt six inches deep in filth, crossed the yard with a bucket of slops. She did not even cast a glance at Aurora.

The windows of Edward's house overlooked Mill Street and Conduit Street. But its rear wall was solid, except for attic windows, which were visible if Aurora stepped back far enough. No one could be watching from inside. She shivered, though the day and her clothes were warm. It was apprehension, she told herself, not fear. What she was about to do did not frighten her. It was a necessity.

A panelled door in a stout frame opened off the narrow part of the alley. Nailed to it was a piece of wood with the word "Deede" carved into it for the benefit of tradesmen, coachmen and messengers such as her disguised self. She climbed the step and knocked. While she waited she tried to picture the Deedes' servants: Harrison, who had taken her cloak and brought water when she had pretended to faint; the young man, Robert, who had helped him wait at table; Missy, who had brought the tea. She thought wistfully of Hester, who had done whatever she was asked for ten years and had still had time to soothe grazed knees, invent rainy-day games and act as mediator in sisterly disputes.

"Yes?" It was Missy. Aurora dipped her chin.

"Message for Mr Deede," she announced, imitating Mary by not using unnecessary words.

"Master, or young master?"

"Young master."

"Who is the message from?"

"Mr Marshall of the sign of the Seven Stars in Covent Garden."

Missy contemplated her with her head on one side. Aurora looked steadfastly at the doorstep, pretending the awkwardness of an inferior servant before a superior one.

"Mr Deede is from home," said the maid. "If you will tell me your master's message I will pass it to him when he returns."

"Master said the message is to be delivered to Mr Deede himself." From her pocket Aurora drew the letter from her sister, which had been the nearest paper to hand when she had changed her clothes. "He was most particular that I put this into his hands myself."

An uncertain look came over Missy's face. "Oh, very well. Mr Marshall should have sent a man-servant, though. Mr Deede will be at White's." And without any parting words, she shut the door.

Aurora hurried away, her brain busy. Joe Deede did not feel the need to practise fencing, then. He would rather spend the day discussing whichever subject arose with anyone who would listen. Everyone talked to everyone else in a coffee house, from aristocrats to journalists, from physicians to booksellers, from attorneys to slave-merchants.

Everyone, that is, except women.

There were plenty of people about, mostly of the middling sort, and mostly men. Nobody looked at Aurora as she approached White's. The door stood open, but a thick fog of tobacco smoke hung between Aurora and proper sight of any of the customers. The place was crowded and very noisy, each voice raised over the din of all the others until every man was shouting. She knew that the only feminine presence would be the woman who operated the steaming, puffing array of coffee pots behind the counter. Ladies did not go into coffee houses, and neither, as Missy had pointed out, did female servants.

She loitered until one of the waiters who carried trays between the tables passed within calling distance of the doorway. "Sir, a word!" she shouted.

The man ignored her. She waited for another, and shouted louder. This time, she was rewarded with a stare. She waited again until an untidily dressed man smoking a pipe came to the door for some air. "Excuse me, sir, but I have an urgent message for a gentleman who might be here. Would you ask him to come to the door?"

The man, who was short, red-complexioned and, Aurora thought, unnecessarily dirty, looked her up and down. "Your mistress send you?"

"No, sir, my master. Please, sir, it is very important, and I must deliver the message personally. Master said."

He continued to leer at her, sucking on his pipe. "And what reward will I receive for my trouble?"

Aurora bobbed another curtsey, her stomach lurching. "Sir, I wish merely—"

"You *wish*!" Offended, the man stared at her. "You should mind your manners, girl." And with that he disappeared back into the gloom.

Aurora stood despondently on the pavement. Her arm throbbed. Longing to sit down, she leaned her right shoulder against the door jamb and peered into the room. A strong mixture of humanity, smoke and coffee grounds attacked her nostrils. No one had swept or dusted for a long time; the rushes strewn on the floor were matted with dirt and spilled drinks. The air away from the door was evidently very hot, for almost all the men were in their shirts and waistcoats, though they all retained their wigs, and some of them their hats. Aurora thought they looked comical, like a crowd of chattering, puff-chested birds, pecking at their drinks.

She stood on tiptoe, hoping to catch sight of Joe over all the heads. She could not see him; he might not be here at all, or he might be in the farther room. Even smokier than the room that opened onto the street, this inner room was lined with tables screened from each other by high partitions. How could she alert him to her presence? No one would help her. No one even noticed her. She was only a servant-girl.

Then she saw him. He walked quickly towards the door, pushing his way between the customers, pulling on a coat with wide, embroidered cuffs. He wore a curled wig and his plumed hat. Aurora was as impressed as ever by the beauty of his countenance. Indeed, now she had witnessed the volatile temperament it concealed, its smooth plausibility was the more astonishing.

He was in deep conversation with another man, young like himself, a stranger to Aurora. They spoke earnestly, their hats almost touching. Neither had seen her. Her courage faltered, but she steadied it. Keeping her head down, she waited in the shadow beneath the overhanging building, ready to step into their path.

The stranger suddenly raised his head in laughter. He spoke low, but Aurora was close enough to hear his words. "Tomorrow we shall drink to the death of a man too stupid to live!"

Joe was smiling, though his voice was full of contempt. "And too stupid to know he has set his murderer free."

"Aye," agreed the other man. He touched his hat. "Until tomorrow," he said to Joe, and the two men shook hands.

"I will bring what I owe," she heard Joe murmur, and then they parted. Joe set off towards Mill Street, the other man more slowly in the opposite direction.

Cold horror spread through Aurora's body. She was too stunned to cry out. Poor, honourable Edward, practising his swordsmanship in some fencing-hall with his loyal friend! He believed that his opponent would abide by the rules of duelling, as a gentleman. But Joe had hired this unknown man not as his second in a duel, but as his accomplice in an assassination. By laying down the challenge, Edward had given Joe Deede the opportunity to kill him without fear of prosecution – he had indeed "set his murderer free".

Her brain racing, she turned in the direction of the Black Swan, as unnoticeable in her maid's garb as the stones on which she trod. How could she warn Edward? She must find him and Richard, wherever they had gone, and tell them of the plot against Edward's life. Her arm had stiffened, but she clasped her hands under her shawl. *Dear God,* she prayed silently as she hurried on, *I thank you for watching over me, and preventing me from stepping forth and revealing myself to Joe Deede. Now, I beseech you, in your almighty wisdom, let me find Edward before it is too late. Heavenly Father, protect my husband from harm!*

Edward and Richard were not at the inn. Aurora again employed Flora's folded letter, taking it from her pocket and imploring the innkeeper to tell her where Mr Hoggart had gone so that she could deliver an important message from her master.

"I know not," he insisted. "I have not seen him today. Now be off with you."

"Is there someone here who *did* see him?"

The man heard the desperation in her voice. He gave her a closer look, and relented. "Out the back," he said, jerking his head. "Nathaniel might have spoken to him."

Nathaniel was a wiry man of about thirty, employed

to feed and water horses and haul casks of ale. He wore a leather apron and filth-encrusted boots. To Aurora's dismay, he did not know which fencing-hall Mr Hoggart had gone to.

"Should never have been fencing at all, if you ask me," he grumbled. "Nasty blow to his head. But that man came … his friend, and—"

"Mr Drayton?" volunteered Aurora eagerly.

"Aye, that be his name. Went off together, they did, about" – he looked at the clock above the stableyard – "must be about two hours ago now."

The clock said a little after four o'clock. Twelve hours from now, unless Aurora could prevent it, two men would draw their swords, one with thoughts of honour satisfied, the other of murder. "Which direction did they go in?" she asked.

Nathaniel considered for a moment, then pointed to his left. "That way. No, I can't be sure."

Aurora's heart dived, but lifted again when the man continued. "I can tell you, though, there is a fencing-hall in Bow Street, hard by the theatre."

"Oh, thank you, sir!"

She set off for Bow Street, her spirits rising. Not only was the fencing-hall near the inn, it was a matter of yards from Mr Marshall's shop. Taking the letter from her pocket once more, she waited by the door until two men came out. But her request met with stares and shrugs. No, they did not know Edward Drayton or Augustus Hoggart. No, they did not know Richard Allcott or Edward Francis. No, they would not go in and enquire.

A boy a few years younger than Aurora emerged from

the fencing-hall. He smiled at her when she stepped forward and listened politely to her words.

"I do not know these gentlemen, but I will return and ask for them," he said pleasantly.

Aurora thanked him, curtseying low, and waited with impatience for Richard or Edward to appear. But only the boy came back.

"Neither of them is here," he told her. "You could try the hall in Duke Street, or the one on the Strand. That one is rather rough, I warn you."

"Miss Drayton" in her silk dress might have persuaded this youth to accompany her, but helpful though he had proved, he was nevertheless of the class that could not associate publicly with a servant. "Thank you, sir, you have assisted me greatly," she said, and watched him walk away.

At Duke Street, she hailed a liveried footman who was about to enter the side door of a grand house. She smiled flirtatiously and he went into the fencing-hall for her. But he too had no luck. And down by the river on the Strand, the fencing-hall was a dark bolt-hole at the bottom of a steep flight of stairs. Everyone who came and went was drunk. Perhaps the boy had been mistaken, and it was not a fencing-hall at all.

Aurora approached a passing couple in the hope that they would look more kindly upon a serving-girl than a man alone "I pray you, sir," she asked the man, "do you know of any fencing-halls hereabouts? I am seeking my master with an urgent message."

He and his lady stopped, and looked at her haughtily. "There is one in Bow Street and another in Duke Street," said the man.

"What of this place, here?" asked Aurora, indicating the dark stairs. "Is this a fencing-hall?" asked Aurora.

"Yes," said the woman, "but *gentlemen* do not fence there."

"Thank you, madam, and you, sir," she said, curtseying to their backs as they hastened away.

Despair closed around her. Edward and Richard were no longer at practice. They had gone somewhere else. She must go back to the rooms above the bookshop, though Edward had said he would not return there before tomorrow, and leave a message with Mary. She must put on her silk gown and leave the same message at the inn. Then, after nightfall, she would wait in St Paul's Church, in case Edward and Richard should decide to ask for God's guidance, and to ask for it herself. If all else failed, she must intercept them on their approach to Lincoln's Inn Fields. She must not give up.

Her plait had escaped from her cap and lay like a rope against her back. Dread had drained her blood from her cheeks, and her injured arm bumped lifelessly at her side as she hurried across the piazza and along Floral Street.

Mary opened the door and gaped at her.

"Mary, it is I!" Aurora took off her hat and cap. "Is Mr Drayton in?"

"No, 'm. Not seen 'im since 'e come in with that pie."

Mary stood back and Aurora stepped into the vestibule. "Then please," she implored the maid, "will you help me change my clothes? I must be quick, and my shoulder…"

"Yes, 'm." Mary had collected herself swiftly and offered a sturdy arm. "Lean on me, if it please you."

Aurora did so gratefully, and they mounted the stairs. The lock had not been repaired; the door swung open.

"Mary, I cannot tell you why I am wearing the clothes of a maidservant," Aurora explained as they entered, "but I must now change into my best dress."

Mary set to work, unbuttoning the front of Aurora's bodice, untying her petticoat. "'Ow did you get this on, with your shoulder an' all?" she muttered.

"Very untidily, I fear," said Aurora. "You are kind, Mary."

Mary made a sound like "Heff!" and continued with her task. When Aurora stood in her chemise and corset, the maid scrutinized her blankly. "Shall I do something to your 'air, Miss?"

"Oh, if you would! Let me dress first, though."

Aurora knelt by her trunk and took out her blue dress. Not allowing herself time to falter, she found the bodice and petticoat, and stood up. "Here, Mary, help me put this on. And my cloak too, that one with the wool lining."

It was difficult not to cry out as Mary, who was not a lady's maid, tied and buttoned the inner garments with blunt, work-worn fingers, then drew the blue silk sleeves over Aurora's arms and fastened the waistband of the skirt. But the result looked neater than Aurora could have achieved alone. "Thank you," she said. "I am sincerely grateful, and will give you something for your trouble if you will hand me my purse."

"No, 'm," said Mary unexpectedly, dropping a curtsey. "I don' expect nothin'. An' if it will please you to sit down, I will brush your 'air."

Unplaited, Aurora's coppery hair lay on her shoulders like strands of seaweed. Mary brushed it and tied the top up with blue ribbons. "Leave the bottom part loose," instructed

Aurora. "Edward ... I prefer it loose around my neck."

"Yes, 'm."

Aurora sensed that Mary longed to know where she could be going that demanded such careful dressing. But how could she confess that she was adorning herself for her husband on what might prove to be the last day of his life? Even if she succeeded in warning Edward, he might still not escape the assassin. And he was still the man who, stubbornly concerned more with his honour than his life, had cast down Aurora's lace-edged glove. His sense of honour might compel him to face Joe Deede in a duel anyway. A duel was a ritual, just as the aftermath of death was a ritual. Aurora must pay homage to those rituals, preserving as much dignity as she could, for herself, for Richard, but most of all for Edward.

"We have been invited to a musical recital in St Paul's Church this evening," she lied as Mary curled locks of hair around her fingers. "Mr Drayton is to meet me there. He loves music."

She should not have said that. It took every ounce of her remaining strength to hide the rush of hard, unforgiving, relentless dread that pushed its way through her body. Her face in the mirror looked white, her eyes glittered. She put her head down. "I thank you, Mary, but I must go now. My hat and gloves are on the bench in the other room."

Mary put her cloak around her shoulders and tied her hat-ribbons for her. But when the maid brought her the lace-edged gloves, Aurora did not put them on. She remembered too vividly her horror when Edward had thrown the right-hand glove down and Joe Deede had picked it up. She would never wear those gloves again. "No, I have changed my mind," she told the maid. "I will wear the plain ones, which are longer, and will keep me warmer in the church. You will find them on the top of my trunk."

Mary fetched Aurora's long gloves and helped her put them on. At the door, Aurora paused. "Mary, would you do something else for me?" she asked.

"Yes, 'm," said Mary, planting her feet, poised to fetch whatever Aurora requested.

"If Mr Drayton should return in my absence, will you tell him I am waiting for him at St Paul's Church, and he *must* come there?"

Mary did not reply, but curtseyed, never taking her eyes off Aurora's face.

"Then I bid you goodnight," said Aurora. She turned to go, then turned back. "There is one more thing. If neither Mr Drayton nor I should return tonight, will you tell Mr Marshall – but *only* Mr Marshall – that messages sent to a Mr Augustus Hoggart at the Black Swan will reach us?"

"The Black Swan," repeated Mary. "A Mr Hoggart."

"That is correct. Thank you."

Aurora went down the stairs and opened the door. Drawing her cloak closer around her shoulders, she stepped out into the shadowy, deserted street.

A Bloodied Blade

Edward and Richard had not returned to the inn.

The innkeeper, who obviously recognized Aurora as the serving-girl who had spoken to him and Nathaniel earlier, kept his counsel. He offered to allow Miss Drayton to wait in his front parlour, but she gave him the message that Mr Drayton must join her in the church of St Paul, impressing its importance upon him as best she could.

He assured her that he would do her bidding. "But if they do not come back here tonight, I cannot help you, Miss Drayton," he told her apologetically. "Gentlemen may do as they please."

"That is true," agreed Aurora, gathering her skirt. "You have done all you can, and I thank you."

Hurrying away, she heard a faraway bell toll nine. She passed the Theatre Royal, its flares burning yellow circles into the twilight, crossed the piazza and stepped into the dim hush of St Paul's Church. If she waited here for Edward in vain, by dawn she would have no choice but to violate the law that banned women from attending duels. The duellists would gather upon Lincoln's Inn Fields before dawn – by four o'clock, Edward had predicted. She would be there in good time. But until then, she would wait in the sight of God.

The glory of the church interior, which usually lifted her spirits, only deepened her distress. Wherever Edward lay tonight, did he truly imagine her to be asleep in their lodgings, numbed by laudanum, resigned to her imminent widowhood? If so, she thought unhappily, she had brought his low opinion of her upon herself.

He had made many declarations of his love for her: as a statement of fact in her mother's drawing room, formally at the wedding breakfast and more passionately when he had confessed his penniless state. She remembered the misery in his voice when she had returned from Drury Lane with news of the attractiveness of Joe Deede. "Do you doubt I love you?" he had asked plaintively. She, may God forgive her, had not even honoured his question with a proper answer. And when he had reminded her in Spring Gardens that it was he, not Joe Deede, who loved her truly, all she had shown him was contempt.

But everything was different now. The way Edward had half smiled, regarding her with such tenderness as she had pleaded with him to call off the challenge, had betrayed his awareness of her feelings. After all his own avowals of love, he had recognized her desire to make one herself. But he had prevented her. If only she had not bowed to his superior prudence! If she had allowed her emotions to overpower her, and had embraced him when she could, he would now know for certain that he was the possessor of her heart, secure in her everlasting love.

But she had not, and he did not know. Now, perhaps, he never would.

She retreated far into the shadows at the sides of the nave, sat in a pew and leaned her head against her clasped hands. She tried to pray, but she was filled with agonizing hopelessness. She got to her feet and walked to and fro between the pews in the near-darkness, each step strengthening her regret.

Her legs trembling, she lowered herself once more into the pew. A long, long time passed. Each opening of the church door, every footstep on the stone floor roused her, and raised her hopes. But in vain The bell in the tower above her rang out ten, then eleven o'clock. At midnight, she gathered her skirt in her right hand and went to the door. An impenetrable darkness had fallen upon Covent Garden.

Aurora shuddered. It was the witching hour, right enough; before the sun rose today, either Edward or Joe would die. *Please God,* she prayed as she closed the door and returned to her seat, *can you not spare them both?*

She was awoken from a fitful sleep by the striking of three o'clock. She struggled to haul herself to consciousness. When she moved, she gasped. Every muscle in her body had stiffened, and her shoulder was shooting bolts of agony down her arm. But she made herself sit up, ignoring the pain, remembering with a jolt of terror where she was.

There was yet time. She must go.

Lincoln's Inn Fields was not far, but as Aurora approached it she felt it might as well be a hundred miles away from the sanctuary of St Paul's. It was, as she had often been told, the last piece of countryside in the great city of London. Criss-crossing paths were the only mark humans had left upon it; the land remained Nature's own. Unlit, the trees untamed, the grass trimmed only by wandering sheep, darkness and loneliness enclosed it utterly.

Aurora was frightened. However profound her distress that Edward faced death, and however fierce her determination to save him from it, fear possessed her. The Fields were larger than she had thought. The darkness was blacker than she had imagined. There was no noise except the occasional rustle in the undergrowth of some nocturnal animal. Supposing the duellists chose another area altogether, behind some trees, or hidden by bushes? Supposing she neither saw nor heard them until it was too late?

Although the dawn was some way off, the intermittent chatter of birds had begun. The creatures were aware of the warming of the air, and the most minute sliver of brightness, far beyond Aurora's senses. The natural world was awakening, and as soon as there was enough light, the duel must be done.

She tried to get her bearings. She had walked northeast from Covent Garden, and she was at the southernmost corner of the Fields. She must find the centre as accurately as she could, for there she would have the best chance of hearing anyone approach, from whatever direction.

The sunrise, though as yet too weak to throw anything but the faintest grey light, aided her. She knew the sun must be due east, so she walked with it on her right, watching for the lumpy shapes of buildings to become visible over the trees, reasoning that when she was about the same distance from any building, in any direction, she must be near the centre.

She came upon a space, apparently deliberately cleared for some sport. Bear-baiting, cock-fighting, she knew not. But here, it was certain, men had gathered, hidden from the world by a thicket of hawthorn and tall elms. She hung back amongst the trees; if they arrived first, Joe Deede and his accomplice must on no account catch sight of her. Stiff with pain and dread, she sank to the grass at the foot of a tree to wait while the world brightened around her and the birdsong gradually increased to a full chorus. Away to the south, she heard a quarter to four strike, and within minutes, heavy treads on the grassy path alerted her to the sight of two men approaching the clearing.

Aurora recognized Joe's plumed hat. He wore no other finery, though. Woollen breeches and sturdy riding boots showed beneath his cloak, and his sword hung at his side in a belt of plain leather. When he spoke to the other man, his breath made clouds in the cold air. Both wore thick gloves, and the accomplice had around his neck a kerchief, the purpose of which, Aurora guessed, was to disguise his face when the moment came. He did not seem to be carrying a sword.

Her stomach lurched. She had eaten nothing since Sunday evening, and Tuesday morning was now dawning. But it was not lack of food that was churning her entrails. It was the knowledge that she beheld, here amongst the trees, her husband's murderer.

She must apprehend Edward before he reached the clearing. But which way would he come? She could not tell, because she did not know where he had spent the last few hours. Her heart drummed; she could not think. It was while she was cowering low beneath the hawthorns, cursing her helplessness, that the unmistakeable sound of horses' hooves, their snorting and blowing, and then the sight of their steaming coats, came near.

Richard must have had horses at the inn. Of course, he owned a carriage, did he not? Had he driven in it to London from Hartford House, when he had brought Flora's letter? Why had Aurora not thought to ask Nathaniel if Mr Hoggart and Mr Drayton had taken *horses*, or Mr Hoggart's *carriage*? Richard and Edward could have been at Hartford House all day, or visited any fencing-hall within twenty miles. Had desperation so affected her brain that this possibility had not struck her?

Edward was more of a horseman than he had implied. He and Richard seemed to have ridden a long way, at a gallop. The horses were panting, and Richard removed his hat to wipe sweat from his face. The bandage round his head showed white in the mist-grey air. Edward dismounted in a swift, practised movement, soothing his horse. His clothes were covered with a dark cloak, and he wore his short wig and an untrimmed hat. He handed the reins to Richard and stood, his head raised, his sword sheathed at his side, watching the movements of Joe Deede and the man he assumed to be Deede's second. Aurora's heart had leapt into her throat. Seeing Edward's breath as he exhaled, she realized with a stab of dismay that hers must be equally visible.

Richard, still mounted, was leading Edward's horse nearer her hiding place. Her cloak over her mouth, unable to attract his attention by calling, she picked up a small stone and threw it at Edward's horse. She was not a very good shot; it landed short. But it disturbed the foliage enough for Richard's head to whip round. He did not signal to Edward or cry out, but slipped quietly out of the saddle, came round to Aurora's side of the horse and, using its body to conceal his action, peered between the bushes.

There was not much light, and her face was shadowed by her cloak and hat. But he *must* see her. "Richard!" she hissed. "Warn Edward!"

Surprise crossed Richard's face, but he crouched, pretending to examine the horse's shoe, and nodded.

"The man with Joe Deede is not his second, but his accomplice!"

He still said nothing, but beneath the shadow of his own hat Aurora saw his jaw stiffen.

"You must believe me, Richard!" she pleaded. "The man is a paid assassin. I had this from Deede's own lips. There will be no duel. You must get Edward away before it is too late."

Men on horseback could readily outpace men on foot. God had done His work. They would surely be saved. But Richard hesitated. "Can you ride?" he whispered.

"No." She understood what was in his mind. "Flee, and do not give thought to me! They are not aware that I know of their plot, and they have not seen me. I will be safe. Now, go!"

To her relief, he stood up. Holding the reins of both horses, he led them into the middle of the clearing, where Edward and Joe faced each other. When Aurora saw that they had already shed their cloaks, and were waiting, swords drawn, for the *en garde* to be called, she had to stuff the edge of her own cloak into her mouth to suppress a shriek.

"What the devil are you doing, man?" Joe's enraged voice boomed in the silence as Richard led the horses into his path. "Get out of the way!"

"Edward!" shouted Richard. "Mount and flee! It is a plot!"

But before Edward could move, Joe Deede ran at him like a madman, his sword aimed at Edward's chest. Richard shouted again, and Edward cast himself sideways onto the ground. Joe's sword caught him a blow below the left shoulder, but Aurora was unable to see, in the tangle of horses and men, how badly he was hurt.

To her horror, the assassin had drawn a short-bladed dagger, which he held aloft as he ran towards Edward. Richard's horse, alarmed by the affray, wheeled round, its hooves churning the earth. One of its back legs struck the man. He fell, cursing mightily, his weapon landing a yard off. He managed to reach it, but Richard had drawn his own sword. "Stay!" he commanded, stern-faced, his sword at the assassin's throat. The man fell back and lay on the ground.

Aurora found herself whimpering. She could not help herself. She watched in horror as Edward leapt to his feet and thrust his rapier at Joe Deede, who had again raised his sword. Each man made another pass; Joe was accurate, but Edward, despite his injury, was agile. Screeching in frustration, Joe made another murderous lunge, but Edward was ready for it. He evaded Joe's blade and, before his opponent could steady himself, ran him through with his own.

Joe sank to the grass, clutching his breast. His wig had fallen off, displaying a short fuzz of hair, the colour of Celia's. It was the first time Aurora had seen him without his wig. He strove to hold up his head, but Aurora could see he had little strength left. Blood had come into his mouth. Before his head finally dropped she heard him splutter the words, "Honoria! My dearest God, Honoria!"

The assassin took advantage of Edward and Richard's motionless horror. With one swift movement he pushed

Richard's sword aside and rose. Secreting his own blade beneath his waistcoat, he made off at a brisk pace between the trees.

"Come, Aurora! Make haste! We must away!"

It was Richard's voice. She felt his hands reach for hers; he pulled her to her feet. "Edward!" was all she could say. "Edward's wound, is it...?"

But Richard was not listening. He was gathering the reins of the horses, who had not bolted, to Aurora's relief, but had merely retreated to the thicket on the other side of the clearing. One was still showing the whites of its eyes in fear, but the other, perhaps more used to witnessing its master's swordplay, was calmer. "Edward!" Richard said sharply to his friend. "You must mount, if you can!"

But Edward still had not moved. He stood above the body of Joe Deede, staring at it in disbelief. "He is dead," he said, "by my hand. I killed him."

Aurora went to his side. His eyes were empty of everything but deep sorrow. He looked at her without love, without relief, almost without recognition. "I killed a man," he repeated. "A man in full health. I am no better than a murderer myself."

She knew it was futile to try and comfort him. He could know no comfort. She turned away, overwhelmed suddenly by confusion and fear. She could look neither at the body of Joe Deede, the man whose feelings she had assumed she was trifling with, nor at Edward, the man whose feelings she *had* trifled with, and whose forgiveness she now so agonizingly craved. Bile rose in her throat; she feared she would vomit.

Richard approached, leading Edward's horse. "Joe

Deede meant to kill you, Edward, regardless of any duel," he said steadily, though Aurora could hear horror in his voice still. "He was not an honourable opponent. You had to defend yourself."

Edward's face was as white as wax. Aurora saw his eyes pinken, as if they were suddenly hot, and tears gather on his lower lids. She had never seen a man cry. "Edward," she said, her voice shaking, "my dear husband, you must come away."

The left side of his shirt bore a bloodstain from the neck to the waist. It was worsening; blood was still flowing from the wound. Aurora picked up his cloak from where he had discarded it on the grass, and put it around his shoulders. He still held the bloodied sword by his side. She grasped the hilt and laid it down, then she took Edward's hand, which was sticky with Joe Deede's blood. Again, nausea attacked her. She fought it, and it withdrew.

"Away!" urged Richard. "Edward, it is done. We must go." He retrieved Edward's sword and, without stopping to wipe it, replaced it in its scabbard. Gently, avoiding his friend's injured side, he steered Edward towards his horse and helped him mount. Then he lifted Aurora and placed her on his saddle. "I have no side-saddle," he told her, "so you must sit astride. But I will ride behind you, you need not fear."

Aurora had never sat upon a horse before. The ground looked a very long way beneath her. But she was not concerned for herself. She could think only of Edward's distress. She clung to the front of the saddle while Richard took the reins to guide the horse out of the clearing. Her eyes were fixed upon her husband, who rode ahead of them, his head bowed, one hand clutching the reins, the other bent lifeless across his body.

Aurora felt Richard's arms enclose her as he mounted the horse. He set it to follow Edward's despondent figure. Aurora's last glimpse of the place touched the body of Joe Deede, lying in a darkening mass of his blood. And at last, she wept.

The room at the Black Swan was full of daylight. Edward lay on Richard's bed with his eyes closed, his face as motionless as a mask. Mercifully, he was no longer bleeding. The stain on his shirt had stiffened and was turning brown.

Richard was sitting on a bench in his shirtsleeves, his face pinched with anxiety. "He will live," he murmured. "It is but a flesh wound. He will live."

Aurora sank to her knees by the bed. The sunlit room blurred into a shifting collection of wet colours. She blinked again and again, trying to push the tears away. "Thank God," she whispered. Her head felt light, with relief and from many hours without food or drink. She took Edward's hand. "Edward…" She could not tell if he had heard her, but she persevered. "It is I, Aurora. I will not leave you. Now, sleep."

"You too must sleep," Richard told her. "You too are injured."

"I cannot sleep. I must keep vigil here. I must watch for signs of fever."

"That is true, indeed. But I can watch." Richard's voice shook. When Aurora turned to him she saw bewilderment on his face. He was still deeply unsettled by the treachery he had witnessed. "You are aware, are you not," he asked, "that if Edward had not been so practised with the rapier, Deede would have pierced his heart?"

Aurora nodded. "Luckily for Edward, Joe Deede did

not practise yesterday. He spent the day at White's."

"He had no need to practise," observed Richard grimly. "Edward was supposed to be murdered before the duel ever began."

Aurora looked at him earnestly. "But Edward's killing of Deede was *not* murder, was it? Edward laid down the challenge to a fair fight, governed by rules. You will bear witness to the fact that Joe Deede thrust illegally, before the *en garde* had been given, will you not?"

"Certainly, but" – Richard sighed resignedly – "I do not think there will be a trial. Deede's body will be taken away by his friends, who will put out that he died honourably in a duel, and Edward will not report what really happened." His troubled eyes searched her face. "We must say nothing, Aurora. One danger has passed, but today's events will give rise to further dangers."

She rose from the bedside and sat beside him on the scarred bench. She lowered her voice. "Richard, what do you understand by Joe Deede's dying words?"

His attention sharpened. "I heard nothing. What did he say?"

"He said, 'Honoria! My dearest God, Honoria!' I heard it plainly, and I believe Edward heard it too."

There was utter silence. Aurora could not hear Edward's breathing, or Richard's, or her own. She could not hear servants going about their work, or horses in the street. It was as if the world had been frozen by an invisible spell. "Do you think it could be to do with Josiah Deede's secret?" she asked. "The one he was blackmailed for?"

Richard frowned, struck by this thought. "It may well be," he observed. "A woman is often at the heart of blackmail."

Aurora asked the question that had been burning in her brain ever since they had left Lincoln's Inn Fields. "Richard, could the blackmailer be Joe Deede?"

Richard frowned more deeply, but said nothing.

"Maybe Joe knew something concerning this woman Honoria, which his father wished to keep secret," continued Aurora. "If it was also known to Henry Francis, Joe might have discovered this and blackmailed his father in Henry Francis's name."

Richard rose and walked up and down the room several times. Then he looked piercingly at Aurora. "Joe Deede's body will have been removed from the Fields and taken to Mill Street by now," he told her. "Josiah Deede knows who Miss Drayton and her brother really are. He knows he is under suspicion of foul play with regard to the death of Henry Francis, and will be on his guard. Do you understand?"

Aurora nodded. "But he does not know what his son's last words were. He may not even know that Joe intended to murder Edward in cold blood. We must use his ignorance, and his grief for his son, to our advantage. We must tell him what Joe said as he died. Surely, under such duress, Josiah will confess to the murder of Henry Francis, and disclose the secret that has cost him so much?"

She waited expectantly for Richard's reply. He did not immediately give it; he seemed in deep thought. But after a moment he roused himself. "He may, if it be God's will."

With fatigue in her legs, pain in her shoulder and dread in her heart, Aurora stood up and opened the door. "Watch over Edward well," she told Richard. "Though it may lead me into I know not what danger, only I can confront Josiah Deede."

Blood Family

The house at Mill Street looked exactly the same. There was no reason for it to have changed merely because one of its occupants was dead. But as Aurora stood on the pavement and gazed up at it, an irrational thought possessed her that it might somehow have been affected by the passing of a young life, even one wasted by hatred. The windows still gleamed, however; the well-polished knocker still shone; the stone step was swept. Life did not stop for grief.

She sighed. The first time she had been in this house, an excited Celia had scampered upstairs ahead of her. She had scorned her father's insistence that she spend her time reading, and Aurora had lied about her "brother's" similar misguidedness. What had she expected that day? She had entered the house fearfully, yet she had soon convinced herself, naïvely perhaps, that Joe Deede and his sister were innocent of their father's crime. Today, as she waited upon the doorstep, with fear again in her heart, naïvety had turned to knowledge. This would surely be a strange meeting.

For a long time no one answered her knock. Then, when she was about to knock again, the man-servant opened the door and gazed at Aurora with watery eyes. "Good afternoon, Miss Drayton," he said.

"Good aftrenoon, Harrison. I am come to pay my respects."

He nodded. "Miss Celia and the master are in the parlour, Miss. Please wait here."

But Harrison did not have a chance to inform his mistress of Aurora's arrival. Celia flew down the stairs so fast she stumbled on the last one. Harrison went to her aid, but she brushed him off. Her near-fall had loosened some of her hair, which tumbled forward in crimped waves every time she tossed it back. "Throw that woman out of my house!" she demanded.

"I wish to offer you my condolences upon the death of your brother," Aurora told her steadily.

Celia took a sharp breath, more like a shriek than a gasp. "Harrison, get rid of her!"

The man stood where he was, uncertain. He heard the hysteria in his young mistress's voice. But he also saw her father advancing down the stairs with a look of thunder.

"Harrison!" ordered Josiah Deede. "Get you to the kitchen and send up tea. Now, Celia, conduct our visitor upstairs and let us have no more of this nonsense. We are bereaved, but that is not Miss Drayton's fault." His dark eyes went to Aurora's face. "Miss Drayton, will you take a cup of tea with us? We are indebted—"

"She is not *Miss Drayton*, Father," interrupted Celia. "She is the wife of that man who has been the cause of all our troubles. That unspeakable villain! How can it be that he yet lives, and Joe is dead? Has God forsaken us?"

Josiah Deede showed none of the astonishment, or

horror, that Aurora had anticipated. Slowly, his face took on a stunned expression: his eyes as still as stones, his mouth unmoving, and every line in his face deeply drawn. If he had not taken a step back, in apparent revulsion, she would have thought it possible that he might strike her.

She maintained a serene countenance, though her heart was thudding. "It is true, sir," she said. "I am indeed the wife of Edward Francis. But my husband is not a murderer."

Josiah Deede's hand was at his throat. He loosened his necktie, and took in several draughts of air. "Why, then, Miss ... er, Mrs Francis, did you pretend to be someone you are not?" he asked in bewilderment.

Aurora thought quickly. If Josiah was truly as ignorant of events as he seemed, Joe had more to answer for even than she had feared. Did his father truly *not know* that "Miss Drayton" had stolen the blackmail letter while acting as Edward's spy? Had Joe found the key, but told Josiah *nothing*? Had the villain, right from the start, been Joe, and Joe alone?

"I was attempting," she told Deede, "on my husband's behalf, to find out more about his disinheritance." Seeing a question flicker across his face, she added hurriedly, "You see, we had reason to suspect all was not as it seemed."

Josiah Deede regarded her with a mixture of suspicion and interest. "Indeed?"

"If you will allow me, sir, I will explain." She glanced at Harrison, who had not yet departed for the kitchen. "Upstairs."

Celia picked up the skirt of her mourning gown and began to mount the stairs. "Then I am going to my room," she announced, "where you may seek me when you have

187

finished talking of matters to which I have no desire to be privy."

Josiah Deede's voice boomed so loudly, and so suddenly, Aurora jumped. "You will stay where you are, madam!"

Celia did not stop. Aurora glanced at the girl's father; his face was no longer stony, but lit by indignation. He had recovered his composure. He stood solidly at the foot of the stairs, once more a man in command of his own household.

"Go into the parlour!" he instructed his daughter.

Celia stopped, but did not turn. Aurora kept her eyes on her back view, unable to suppress the tight, nervous distrust that crept over her. Joe might have told his father nothing, but how much had he told his sister?

"Celia!" bellowed Josiah Deede. "I am your father and you will obey me!"

Stiffly, as if an invisible force were pushing her against her will, Celia mounted the remaining stairs, crossed the landing and opened the parlour door. Josiah nodded curtly to Aurora. "Excuse this discourtesy. My daughter is distracted by her brother's sudden death. Now, let us go and join her."

"Very well, sir."

As she preceded him up to Edward's mother's pretty, old-fashioned parlour, every sinew of Aurora's body remained alert. She strained to understand Josiah Deede's treatment of her – not, as she might have expected, with the same contempt as Celia, but as a guest, the reason for whose visit he wished to hear. When confronted by the revelation she was about to make, would he turn on her in wrath and accusation? Or not? This was a strange meeting, indeed.

Celia had not sat down. She stood before the empty fire

basket, the back of her head reflected in the mirror above the mantel. She had tidied her hair, but her lovely face was distorted with weeping. "This woman's husband killed Joe, Father!" she blurted.

"That is true, sir," said Aurora before Josiah could speak. "But lawfully, in a duel." She kept her eyes upon Celia. "I witnessed it."

"And you have the effrontery to come here while Joe yet lies upstairs?" retorted Celia. "Shameful!"

Aurora could imagine the incense-filled bedroom where Joe's body would lie on a bier, surrounded by candles and watched over by a priest. Her throat constricted at the thought; at her father's funeral she had been repelled by the accoutrements of death. Tension racking her body, she stood her ground. "Celia, I came because I have an urgent message for Mr Deede from my husband. It will not wait."

"Is your husband too cowardly, then, to deliver the message himself?" asked Celia scornfully.

"No," replied Aurora. "I have come because he is unable to rise from his bed. Your brother wounded him in the shoulder."

"Then your husband should have ended it there." Celia's voice faltered on the last word, and she sat down, plucking distractedly at her skirt. "They should have fought to first blood, and no more. If they had done so my brother would still be alive."

Josiah Deede had listened to this exchange in resigned silence. He took Celia's place before the mantelpiece, resting one hand upon it, and studied Aurora's face with interest. "Mrs Francis," he began, "you say you witnessed Joe's death. Although I am nonplussed as to how you were present at the duel, I beg you, will you tell me truthfully what happened?"

Aurora hesitated, considering her reply. If he truly was innocent of Joe's murderous plan, she could not tell him she went to the duelling place in order to warn her husband of it. "Very well, sir, I will recount events as I saw them," she began. "Joe advanced and wounded my husband. I hoped that would be the end of it, and they would but fight to first blood as your daughter suggests. But he advanced again, and Edward was obliged to defend himself."

"Were there no seconds present?" asked Josiah, frowning.

"There were indeed, sir. Edward's friend Mr Allcott was his second, and Joe also brought a man."

Josiah Deede digested this. "But Joe was intent on fighting to the death, and no one intervened?"

"That is what I saw," said Aurora warily.

She had tried to spare his feelings as far as she could, but nothing could sugar over the fact that Edward had been obliged to kill Josiah Deede's son in self-defence.

He gestured for Aurora to sit, then sank into the armchair. His sumptuous mourning clothes – a black waistcoat embroidered with jet and a long coat trimmed with sable – made deep folds around him. A sigh began within him, rose shuddering to the surface and subsided.

"Look at my father!" demanded Celia, flinging out a slender arm. "Look at him, robbed of his only son by your husband's blade! Where is your compassion, *Mrs Francis*? Have you not eyes to see, nor heart to feel his despair?"

"Peace!" said Josiah. "Peace, child!" He spread his hands in a calming motion, closing his eyes and opening them again. "Let us hear what message Mrs Francis has brought.

She herself is guilty of nothing more than concealing her identity."

"Thank you, sir," said Aurora. She sat down. Her heartbeat had calmed, but her jaw felt stiff as she continued. "Edward wishes you to know that your son spoke the name of a woman just before he departed this earth."

Beneath the grey mask of grief, Aurora caught the sharpening of Josiah's expression. She was not looking directly at Celia, but she was aware that the girl had grown very still, no longer worrying her skirt, but sitting as if she were in church, her hands folded in her lap.

Aurora gathered her courage. "He cried out, 'Honoria!'," she told Josiah. "'My dearest God, Honoria!'"

Nothing happened. Celia went on sitting in the same position, and her father continued to look at Aurora with undivided attention. The only difference she could discern in his face was a slight flaring of his nostrils, as if to increase his intake of air.

"Is this name familiar to you, Mr Deede?" ventured Aurora. She glanced at Celia. "Or to you?"

Still Celia did not move, but her eyes followed her father as he rose from his chair and went to the window. The light of the May afternoon brightened the embroidery of his waistcoat and gleamed on his forehead and nose. His eyes blinked steadily. "It is many, many years since I heard that name," he said, so quietly that Aurora could hardly hear him. "I never thought to hear it again. And certainly not from my son."

"Who is this Honoria, Father?" asked Celia.

Aurora again felt, without tangible cause, that Celia was not trustworthy. Celia had lied to her before, but she had not discerned it, perhaps because at the time she was engaged in trying to make her own lies plausible. But now, in the presence of her grief-stricken father, and separated for ever from Joe, Celia's power to deceive had diminished.

There was a knock, acknowledged impatiently by Celia. Harrison and Missy entered, bearing the kettle and tea tray as usual. No one spoke while the servants were in the room. As soon as the door had closed behind them, Josiah sighed deeply. Without turning from the window, he said, "Honoria was Edward Francis's mother."

Aurora knew that Edward's mother's name had been Elizabeth. Her heart drummed, but she said nothing.

"She was the first woman I loved, when I was a young man of twenty-six," Josiah continued. "But she was one of King Charles's mistresses, and refused to marry me. In sixteen seventy-five, she had a son – not the king's, but mine." Beneath straight brows his eyes alighted upon Aurora, whose breath had disappeared. "Mrs Francis, *I* am Edward's father."

Celia's blue eyes looked blank, but she remained composed. Her only betrayal of agitation was to put her hand to her throat. "Do you mean that Edward Francis, that murderer…" she began faintly, but was prevented from continuing by her father's next words.

"Honoria could not risk the wrath of King Charles," he went on, addressing Aurora. "He would have dismissed her from court if he had discovered she had betrayed him. So she surrendered the child to me to find a family for him. I was scarce out of the University, with only my profession to support me. But my friend Henry Francis came from a landed family and had recently married a wealthy woman.

They took the boy in and raised him as their own. Honoria did not wish to be told of his whereabouts, and now she, too, is dead."

Aurora still could not breathe satisfactorily. She grasped the arm of her chair, fearing faintness would overcome her. Joe Deede's wickedness was almost beyond reckoning. Somehow, he must have found out about Honoria. He must have known that he had an older half-brother who would inherit his father's fortune if his parentage became known. So he decided to make sure Edward's parentage did *not* become known, by fuelling the enmity between Josiah Deede and Henry Francis. First, he had blackmailed Josiah in his former friend's name. Then he had robbed Edward of his fortune by murdering his adoptive father. And then, when Edward had given him the opportunity by challenging him to a duel, he had decided to kill him.

"But Father..." said Celia. Her face had taken on a dazed expression. "All my life, you have hated Henry Francis. Joe and I were always kept away from his son."

"Your mother insisted, and so did Henry," replied Josiah, returning to his chair. "But differences over religion were only a small part of my estrangement from him. Our greatest quarrel was over Edward. When the boy was ten years old, King Charles died, and King James ascended the throne. For those of the Roman faith, everything at court changed. Because I had converted when I married my Philomena, I now found myself favoured by the Catholic king. My wealth exceeded that of Henry Francis, and I wanted my boy back, to bring him up as a Catholic and my own son."

"But what about *Joe*?" protested Celia. "Expecting all his life to inherit as the only son, then having to surrender his fortune to an elder brother he did not even know about!"

Her indignation was not very convincing, Aurora thought. Celia knew, she *knew*.

"That would not have happened, Celia," said Josiah. "You see, your mother would only agree to take the boy if I willed the estate to Joe, though he was the younger son, while making good provision for Edward. And I have never changed that arrangement."

Celia had turned paler. She looked at the floor, her eyes widening. Evidently, she had not known *this*.

"Everything was planned," continued Josiah. "But Henry refused to give up the boy, and I allowed my disappointment to turn to loathing. I am ashamed to say I caused things about Henry Francis to circulate in society which were quite without foundation."

Aurora found her voice, though it did not sound quite as usual. She did not seem able to summon her strength. Whatever she had expected, it had not been this. "Edward's reputation is similarly tainted, I believe," she ventured.

"Aye, I gave Joe free rein to insult him, may God forgive me." Josiah leaned forward and put his elbows on his knees. Aurora recognized the position Edward so often adopted, along with the drawing-together of the eyebrows. "And he took full advantage. But I wonder, Mrs Francis … how did Joe know the name of Honoria?"

Aurora spoke as considerately as she could. "Sir, may I put to you the possibility that Joe came across some private paper which perhaps contained the truth about Edward's parentage?"

He looked at her. Distraction had become grief, descending over his face like a shroud. "Madam, you are perceptive. Such a paper does exist." His voice was low, and the emotion in it was controlled. "It is the agreement Henry and I signed when he adopted him. I could not prevail upon Henry to raise Edward as a Catholic, of course. But I made him agree to certain stipulations pertaining to the boy's education." His eyes found Celia's bowed head and lingered there. "I kept the document hidden," he said, more to himself than to her. "But not well enough, it seems."

He straightened up and rested his head against the chair back. He continued to look at Celia, whose expression was not visible. She remained as still and silent as a statue.

Aurora waited a few moments, then continued. "If Joe found this document, sir, he may have assumed that if the truth about Edward's birth ever became known, the Deede fortune would be bequeathed to Edward, as he was the elder. But you have just informed me that you had no intention of leaving Edward your entire fortune, and upon your wife's insistence you made good provision for Joe."

"That is correct," said Josiah softly. Realization began to glow in his eyes. "Dear God!" he murmured, stricken. "Do you mean that, although Joe may have found the adoption agreement, he never found my will, which stipulates that a very generous portion of my fortune would go to him? He must have assumed, as Celia did just now, that it would all go to Edward!"

"Very likely, sir," said Aurora.

Josiah nodded miserably. "All the copies of my will are kept under lock and key in a cabinet at my attorney's office, to which Joe could not be privy." He gave a heartfelt sigh. "I am to blame. I should have told him and Celia the truth years ago."

Celia's head came up at last, her beauty blunted by indignation. "Father, stop! What have *you* done that could be amiss?"

"Plenty, my dear," said Josiah resignedly. "When I received the first blackmail letter, I knew I could stop Henry Francis's villainy by admitting the truth. Oftentimes, I was sorely tempted to do so, and rid myself of the burden – not the financial burden, but the weight on my heart. But I was too proud, so I paid him."

"Oh, Father!" Celia's exclamation was not one of sympathy, but of contempt. "You could not have done that! A Protestant woman? A bastard son? Mother could never have gone into society again. And how would *I* ever have got a suitor?"

Her father gazed at her, seeing her self-centredness, perhaps for the first time. "Celia," he said solemnly, "there is no need to scold me. It was to protect you, your mother and Joe – and my own pride, as I have said – that I paid. I was not strong enough to confess, and I have scolded myself for it often enough."

"Any man in your position would have done the same," insisted Celia. "It is not a question of strength, but of prudence."

Josiah Deede regarded her sorrowfully. "Very well, my dear," he said, putting his handkerchief to his eyes.

Aurora waited while he composed himself, then she ventured on. "Sir … I regret having to ask such a question, but when Henry Francis disinherited Edward and left his fortune to you, did you not wonder that he could treat his beloved adopted son in such a cruel way?"

Before Josiah could speak, Celia gave a snort of

scorn. "Father, it is perfectly obvious why he disinherited Edward Francis. Because he was *your son*, and he hated you! 'Beloved adopted son', indeed! He must have seen his enemy every time he looked at him!"

Josiah breathed in and out, and wiped his eyes. "I am sorry, Celia," he said, "but I cannot agree. Henry *did* love Edward, and his disinheritance of him is something that has ever mystified me."

"Why, then, sir," asked Aurora solemnly, "did you not protest at the time? Edward contested the will, but the hearing was presided over by Sir John Wilkinson, a judge known to be harsher on Protestant plaintiffs than Catholic ones, and a good friend of you and your circle."

The word "corruption" hung unspoken in the air. Aurora wondered if she had gone too far. She readied herself to receive the full force of Josiah Deede's outrage.

"Hatred, my dear Mrs Francis," he said calmly, "is not easily set aside in favour of compassion, or even logic. I understood Henry's desire to acquit himself of his sins, but I did not understand why he had done it at Edward's expense. However, such was my resentment of both father and son, I made no attempt to give Edward a fair hearing. As I stood there with Joe at the will-contesting, my own will lay locked in my attorney's office. How could I admit in public that Edward was actually *my* son, and that although he might be disinherited now, part of my own fortune would come to him in due course? It would have been the sensation of the year, and my reputation would have been ruined. So I kept my counsel."

Aurora considered, her heartbeat quickening. Josiah's dilemma had not moved her – his stubborn refusal to help his own son was repugnant – and his persistence in believing Henry Francis to be a blackmailer incensed her.

"Sir, Henry Francis did not blackmail you," she told Josiah. "He *could not* have written those letters. For the last ten years of his life, he was unable to write, so crippled were his fingers with rheumatism."

Josiah Deede nodded slowly, the skin around his eyes folding as he gazed at something invisible. "Indeed," he murmured.

He seemed so distracted Aurora could not be sure he had understood. But she pressed on. "And if he dictated them, why has the person he dictated them to not continued with the blackmail himself? I will tell you why. Because the blackmailer wanted you to think he *was* Henry Francis, writing with his own hand, the lone possessor of the secret. When Henry died, they ceased."

Josiah's distraction turned to disbelief, which gradually turned to horror. In the darkest recesses of his eyes, Aurora saw the truth dawn. "Mrs Francis," he gasped, his handkerchief again at his mouth, "what are you suggesting?"

Aurora did not speak.

"Surely," he went on, "the only person who knew about Edward's true parentage, apart from Henry, myself and three deceased women, was ..." – Josiah's expression turned to one of agony – "*Joe?*"

Celia could remain silent no longer. She turned her blue eyes, heavy with weeping yet bright as jewels, upon Aurora. "What nonsense! How dare you accuse my brother of such wickedness?"

"I have accused him of nothing more than rifling through your father's papers," replied Aurora. "Do you believe he could be guilty of more than this?"

"He is innocent of everything!" Celia's eyes implored her father. "Father, it is plain that Henry Francis blackmailed you and changed his will in order to save himself from damnation. All this talk of rheumatism is lies. I cannot fathom how Joe knew this woman Honoria's name, but I swear before God that he was entirely ignorant of Edward Francis's true parentage. And until now, so was I."

Josiah had lifted his head, but Aurora could see that he was barely listening to his daughter's protests. "Dear God," he murmured, his black eyes moving rapidly, seeing nothing, "if Henry was not the blackmailer, there was no need for him to make reparation for what he had done. So why in the name of heaven did he alter his will?"

Aurora's heart thudded, but she kept her nerve. "He did not, sir," she declared steadily. "Someone else did."

No one spoke. Aurora was aware of the sunlight, the silence, Josiah's stunned stare and Celia's horrified one. The room seemed stifling, as if full of some heavier substance than air. The pain in Aurora's shoulder had intensified. She shifted in her chair, trying in vain to ease it. Her mouth was dry. She swallowed, and continued.

"Sir, I was witness to the sword fight, and I was also witness to the challenge, last Sunday night."

Josiah was still staring at her coldly. She pressed on.

"Joe accused Henry Francis of blackmailing you." Her voice wavered as she spoke her next words. "And then … forgive me, sir, but Edward accused you of murdering Henry Francis and altering his will in order to steal his fortune."

There was a silence, during which Aurora heard a low snort of contempt from Celia. Ignoring it, Josiah set his jaw.

"And will you now make the same accusation to my face, Mrs Francis?"

"No, sir," replied Aurora readily.

"And what is preventing you?"

"Honoria herself," explained Aurora. "The woman you once loved, who gave birth to Edward. Now I know your story, I am convinced that you would not commit such a heinous crime against the man who brought up your son."

Josiah gave an almost-imperceptible nod. Aurora kept her eyes on his face, though on the edge of her vision she saw Celia's body stiffen.

"Edward was wrong," she continued. "You are not his father's murderer, and I offer my heartfelt apologies for suspecting you. But whoever *did* kill Henry Francis altered his will that same day, the twelfth of December last. They forged the signature of the witness, dating it six months before, because Lord Snaresborough was killed in an accident in June."

Josiah Deede's deep-set eyes regarded Aurora with a darkness greater than sorrow, greater than suspicion. "So…" he began slowly, "you are saying that Joe took this desperate measure, resorting to murder in order to steal Edward's fortune?"

Aurora nodded. "He thought – wrongly, as it turns out – that he was going to lose his fortune to Edward upon your death," she said. Then she added, hoping to comfort Josiah, "Perhaps there is a misguided logic in that."

But Josiah could not be comforted. He could not go on. He had exhausted his ability to bear the pain, first of his confession and now of this revelation. The burden of Edward's true parentage had weighed heavily upon his heart for many years. Even now that he had confessed, he felt no relief. And now, to hear his other son accused of both blackmail and murder was too much.

Aurora watched as he rose shakily, putting a hand on the window frame to steady himself. In vain. His knees gave way, and he began to sink towards the floor, his long coat splaying around him.

"Father!" cried Celia, and jumped up. As she did so, a small cylindrical object rolled across the floor towards Aurora. She retrieved it, intending to offer it back to Celia, who had evidently dropped it. But when she saw what it was, she slipped it into her pocket.

Celia knelt by her father's side as he lay on the floor, his legs folded awkwardly beneath him, his wig sliding off, his head cradled in his daughter's arms. "Fetch Harrison!" she ordered Aurora.

"Very well," said Aurora, "but if your father is unwell, I can go for a physician. Perhaps if you loosen his necktie—"

"Leave us!" cried Celia bitterly. "He is unwell because *you* have broken his heart!"

Aurora stood back and gathered her skirt. "Even so," she told Celia, "it does not mean I cannot be concerned for him. I have no wish to harm him, as you are well aware."

Celia did not reply. Helplessness and dread silenced Aurora too. With no word of farewell, she turned her back, opened the door and hurried downstairs. "Harrison!" she called in the direction of the kitchen. "Come to your master! Quickly!"

When the man came running, hauling on his coat, she lifted the latch on the front door and let herself out. Once her feet were on the cobbles, she too began to run.

The Power to Work Magic

The apothecary held the phial to the small amount of light that filtered through the coloured bottles and jars in his shop window. "May I ask where you obtained this, sir?"

Richard indicated Aurora, who stood beside him. "This lady found it."

"In the street?" asked the man, regarding Aurora suspiciously.

"No, sir, in a private house," she replied.

He could see she was not inclined to elaborate, and his professional discretion would not allow him to question her further. "The container is the type in which poisons are stored," he observed.

"So we thought," said Richard. "That was our reason for bringing it to you. We wish to know what poison it is, and what its effects are."

The apothecary gave a weary smile and put the phial down on the counter. "Ah. So you intend, sir, to murder your wife and marry your mistress?"

Aurora's legs felt weak. The physical discomfort of a few snatched hours of sleep in a church pew, a long time without nourishment, the exertion of running from Mayfair to Covent Garden and the tumultuous events of the last twenty-four hours were taking their toll. She wished she could sit down, but there was no room in the tiny shop for a chair.

"I take it you are in jest, sir," said Richard in his solemn way. "We merely desire the identification of this substance, for private reasons. If we had illegal intentions we would hardly present ourselves to you as being in possession of it."

Aurora's weariness made her impatient. "That is one of the services apothecaries such as yourself advertise, is it not?" she asked the man. She took a shilling from her purse and slid it across the counter. "I beg you, bring your professional knowledge to bear upon our questions, and be done with it."

The man adjusted his spectacles, removed the stopper from the phial and poured a small amount of the dirty-white powder it contained onto a metal tray. Wetting his finger, he tasted a particle of it. "Arsenic," he announced. "Used for killing rats." He pointed to a large jar on a high shelf, half full of the same greyish-white substance. "It is a common-enough purchase. Indeed, it has often been observed that throughout history it has killed more people than rats, because it is such a convenient poison. It has medicinal and cosmetic uses, it is almost tasteless and odourless, and small doses may be administered over a long period. Furthermore, the symptoms caused by the fatal dose may be confused with other, more natural, deaths."

Richard and Aurora were both staring at him. Aurora's jaw was so tense she could not speak.

"Cholera, for example," the apothecary went on,

scraping up the powder with a tiny spoon and depositing it back in the phial. "Or even an extreme bilious attack, perhaps caused by bad food."

Aurora remembered Edward's description of his father's death: *The physician declared him dead from a convulsion, or from eating something bad.*

Richard put his elbows on the counter and leaned forward, his expression so intense the man took a step back. "So a man might be poisoned, but his death declared a natural one by a physician?"

"Certainly." The man wiped his hands on his apron, watching Richard warily. "The circumstances of the victim's death are often very suspicious."

"Indeed," agreed Richard. He held his hand out for the phial. "We are indebted to you, sir. Would you be so good as to note down the day and date we entered your shop, and what we brought with us? We cannot leave it here, but your recollection of today's events might be very important."

"In a legal situation?" asked the man, placing the shilling in his apron pocket.

"Perhaps."

"Not for the first time." He took writing paper from a drawer and dipped a quill in the inkpot on the counter. "On the afternnon of the tenth of May, seventeen hundred," he said as he wrote, "a lady and a gentleman ..."

"Mrs Francis and Mr Allcott," supplied Richard. "Two *l*s and two *t*s."

"... brought me a phial of a powder which I identified as arsenic. They then took it away with them. Is that all, sir?"

Richard looked at Aurora. She nodded, and he turned

back to the man. "Will you copy it, and give us the copy?"

The man did so. Richard gave him another shilling and requested that the paper be sealed and put away carefully. When he was satisfied, he put the phial and the copy in his pocket, thanked the apothecary again and ushered Aurora from the shop.

The assault of the daylight made her blink. Richard had set off at a smart pace, but she could not match it. He turned back, his face full of apology. "You are weary, I know … forgive me." Then he brightened. "I am in haste to return to Edward. But you know, Aurora, I have somewhere else to go today, have I not?"

She did not know. At least, she could not remember. She shook her head.

"I am going to Dacre Street," he reminded her. "To deliver your letters to your mother and sisters."

"Oh, Richard!" She clutched his arm. "Pray God this may be the last time we must deceive them!"

Edward slept for a long time.

The afternoon became the evening, and the candles were lit, and still he did not stir. Aurora kept vigil beside the bed, every so often reaching out to lay her hand lightly upon his forehead. She was near sleep herself, and her left arm was too painful to move. But each time her chin dropped, the vision of a tall, fair-haired, blue-eyed man flailing his murderous sword jerked her awake.

She looked at her husband. His face was turned three-quarters from her, towards the window, his hair sticking up at the crown. But even in sleep he did not look untroubled. It was not yet over; peace had not come.

St Paul's Church clock struck nine o'clock, and as Aurora watched Edward in the candlelight, he awoke. He looked blankly at the window of the inn room with its shabby drapes and half-open shutters. Then he turned to Aurora, and his eyes cleared.

She reached over and felt his brow. It was cool.

"I am hungry," he announced.

"Then I will order some supper." She rose. "Richard will be returned from Westminster by now. Shall I ask him to join us?"

"Of course."

He put out his hand. "Thank you, my dearest Aurora."

Her heart filled with such a rush she felt her eyes prickle. She blinked. "I will bring him."

She descended the stairs, cradling her arm, and hailed an apron-clad boy who was trudging across the flagstones with a tray of glasses. "Will you bring soup and bread, and some wine, to Mr Hoggart's room?"

The parlour of the inn was good-sized, well lit and crowded. Aurora was met by the sound of chattering voices and the fragrance of roasted meat. It seemed a very long time since she had eaten.

"What news?" asked Richard, half rising from his seat in the inglenook.

"He has no fever," replied Aurora, gesturing for him to sit and sliding in beside him. "He requests food, and your company."

Richard's eyes closed in a brief moment of gratitude to God. "But he remains ignorant of Deede's confession, and his true parentage, does he not?" he asked.

Aurora nodded. She had thought of little else during her

vigil. "I am resolved to tell him myself, as soon as he has partaken of some food."

"And you are adamant Josiah Deede is innocent?"

"Yes," she replied with conviction. "I have been thinking about it. The murder was planned and executed by Joe and Celia. Joe must have exerted force over their victim, while she administered the poison. Her protestations of her brother's innocence, and her declaration that she knew nothing of Honoria, were false. Celia Deede is an accomplished deceiver, even of her own father."

Richard pondered in silence. Aurora glanced at him; the lines of his face were drawn ever more sharply, and his whole frame drooped as he sat on the narrow bench. The man was exhausted.

"Richard," she said gently, "you must rest. When you have seen Edward, return to Hartford House and sleep. You have done everything you can. I am Edward's wife. I will take care of him."

Richard sighed, looked at her for a moment and nodded. "Very well. But you must allow me to do one more thing."

"What is that?"

"I will arrange with the innkeeper for Mr Drayton to stay in Mr Hoggart's room for as long as he needs, and for Miss Drayton to have her own room. I will settle the charges. And Edward cannot walk far, so I will leave my carriage here at the inn for you to use."

Aurora pressed his hand. "I thank you from my heart. But ..." – she felt her colour rise – "I do not think I will have need of the other room. I mean, I must keep watch over Edward."

"Of course," said Richard solemnly.

"Now, let us go to him," said Aurora, avoiding his gaze. "And on the way, you can tell me how you found them all at Dacre Street."

"They are quite well," he told her as they quitted the parlour. "Flora and Eleanora were full of questions, especially about the injury to my head, but your mother had the good sense to discourage them. Kindly, of course."

They are quite well, thought Aurora. Quite well in their ignorance, for now. She shrank from the thought of the battalion of questions she would face when she was at last able to tell them the truth. "Thank you," she said. "You know, Richard, it is a strange thing. When I lived at Dacre Street I felt as if I were in a prison made of gossip and petticoats. I longed for … adventure, I suppose. But since I have left the place, my thoughts of it have grown fonder with each passing day." They had reached the chamber door. Aurora put her hand on the latch. "Am I a shallow, changeable girl, do you think?"

Richard's eyes smiled, though his face remained grave. "You are a girl who loves her family. And who has, perhaps, had enough of adventure?"

"Perhaps," said Aurora, opening the door. "For the time being."

Edward's eyes were closed, but he was not asleep. Watching his friend's face keenly, Richard went to the bedside. "Thank God," he said, and knelt.

Edward opened his eyes and smiled thinly in acknowledgement. "Have you come to take supper with us, Richard?" he asked.

"I thank you, but I am come to bid you farewell,"

replied Richard, rising to his feet. "I must return to Hartford House. Though with God's grace we will all be together again in happier circumstances before long."

"Amen," said Edward. "I cannot embrace you, Richard, but be assured you have my humblest gratitude, from my heart."

"And mine," added Aurora.

Richard nodded. Surreptitiously, he drew out the phial of arsenic and the folded paper from the apothecary, and passed them to Aurora. "I will leave these in your safekeeping," he murmured.

Aurora secreted them in her skirt pocket, into which her mother had sewn buttons and buttonholes, as a precaution against pickpockets. When Richard proffered his hand, she shook it warmly. "God speed."

With a final look at Edward, Richard pulled the door open and left the room, his footsteps thudding quickly on the stairs.

"I could not embrace Richard, and I cannot embrace you," said Edward ruefully.

Smiling, Aurora gently touched his hand. "You may embrace whomever you wish when you are recovered."

There was a knock. It was the serving-boy, bearing a laden tray. "Set it down on the table," instructed Aurora. "And will you ask the chambermaid to bring a pallet, and pillow and blankets?" Fumbling in her pocket for coins, her fingers touched the cold glass of the phial. She wondered if, by now, Celia had missed it.

The boy bowed and disappeared. Taking one of the bowls of soup and a piece of bread, Aurora went to her seat beside the bed. "Edward, I have brought food."

He had not the strength to sit up, so Aurora placed her good arm behind his shoulders and raised him far enough to enable her to place soup-soaked bread in his mouth. The taste of the food gradually improved his demeanour. Aurora watched with relief as he chewed and swallowed with increasing appetite, and colour returned faintly to his cheeks.

By the time she set to her own bowl, the soup was cool, but she devoured it and wiped the bowl with her bread. She made Edward as comfortable as she could against the pillows, then poured two glasses of wine. She sat beside him and took his hand. "There is news I must tell you," she ventured, watching his face. "It is of great import."

Edward frowned. "What day is it today?"

"It is Tuesday."

"Tuesday," he repeated. "The same day that I killed Joe Deede, or another Tuesday?"

Aurora caressed his hand. "The same day. It is evening. You have slept for many hours and lost track of time. But yes, early this morning you went to fight a duel but were obliged to defend yourself against an assassin."

He nodded, still unsure. "This morning?"

"Yes, this morning." She paused, allowing him to absorb this. Then she tightened her grasp on his hand a little, and steadied her nerve. "Edward, did you hear what Joe Deede said as he died?"

His eyes settled upon her face with a questioning look. "Did he say ... a woman's name? Or was that my imagination?"

"It was not your imagination. He said the name 'Honoria'."

"Ah." His gaze left her face and roamed restlessly around the room. "Honoria."

Aurora wished she could leave him to sleep in peace. But though her heart quailed, she knew that no more time should pass without his hearing the truth. "Edward," she began, "I did not know then of whom Joe was speaking. I had never heard of Honoria, any more than you have. But a great deal has happened while you were asleep. I went to Mill Street, and I have found out who Honoria is. Or *was*, as she is no longer living."

Edward heard the shortening of her breath. His eyes fixed upon hers. "And who was she?"

"She was your mother," said Aurora.

His gaze remained upon her face. She watched as surprise, bewilderment, questioning, distrust and, finally, understanding of a sort came in turn to his eyes.

"My *real* mother?" he asked warily.

Aurora nodded. "The woman you knew as your mother, Elizabeth, and the man you knew as your father, Henry, adopted you at birth and brought you up as theirs," she explained. "But your real parents are Honoria, who was a mistress of King Charles, and her lover ..."

She felt his hand grip hers, and he tried to raise himself off the pillows. *"Josiah Deede!"* he finished for her in astonishment. "It cannot be! That murderer cannot be my father!"

"Fear not," Aurora assured him warmly. "Josiah is *not* a murderer. He is as great a victim of his children's villainy as you are."

The colour had gone from Edward's face. Aurora could not imagine how her story must be affecting him. The physical discomfort in his shoulder must be as nothing to the distress in his heart. But as she watched his face, she saw understanding trickle across it. "So Joe Deede …"

Aurora nodded. "… was the blackmailer. And he was your father's murderer. Or at least, he was complicit in his murder." She leaned forward, ready to soothe him lest he become agitated. "Edward, there is more."

He stared at her, his face as still as a mask.

"Celia denied to her father's face that Joe could be guilty of any wrongdoing," she continued. "She defended him vehemently, and she also denied that she herself knew about Honoria. But she was lying, Edward! I am sure of it. She was trying to protect herself, now that Joe is dead. But the truth is that she and Joe had assumed – wrongly, in fact – that if the truth were discovered, their inheritance would be passed to you. Then, if you should die, to me."

She paused. The only sounds were of the ticking of the clock in the corner of the room, and Edward's shallow breathing. He was listening intently. Aurora felt in her pocket for the phial of arsenic. "A few minutes after I was shown upstairs," she continued, "tea was brought, but before Celia could serve it, Josiah told me that he had made provision for you in his will, though most of his fortune was to be left to his children. *I am convinced Celia had no knowledge of this until that moment.* Then Josiah collapsed, overcome, and the tea was abandoned anyway. But when Celia rushed to help him, she dropped this."

She took out the little glass phial and the apothecary's note. As Edward read the paper, every muscle in his face stiffened.

"I was about to give it back to her," added Aurora

gently, "but decided I had better keep it."

Edward sank back against the pillows. "Good God, Aurora!" he said, his voice full of disbelief, sorrow and grief. "How everything now becomes clear!"

"Celia was Joe's accomplice," continued Aurora. "He must have confided in her when he found the document Josiah told me about today, which he and Henry Francis signed upon your adoption. Joe used it first to extort money from Josiah, and then to gain a fortune that was not his own. Now all that is left is to see that Celia is tried for the murder." She held up the phial. "She thinks she has got away with it, but she is mistaken."

He gripped her hand. "You cannot go back there alone!"

"I have no intention of doing so. I will go with representatives of the law and have her arrested."

"No!" His face was stricken. "She will hang!"

"Yes, she will." Suddenly, Aurora understood. "Oh, Edward … she is your sister!"

"If she hangs," he said faintly, as if struggling to get the words out, "my family will be for ever disgraced, and my father – my blood father, Josiah Deede – ruined. Even the return of my fortune will not compensate for such misery. I cannot inflict it."

Aurora was dismayed. "But what of the honour of your *adoptive* family, which you have laboured to defend – even to the point of fighting a duel!" she protested. "That will surely only be preserved if the murderer is exposed?"

"The murderer," said Edward steadily, "is dead."

So he wished to let the dead bury the dead. Josiah Deede would remain innocent of his daughter's complicity in his son's crimes. Edward's fortune would be returned, and Celia, still a rich woman, would marry an equally rich man of the Roman faith and remain unpunished for the rest of her life. Aurora strove to understand her husband's wishes. "You are magnanimous," she said.

When she looked at him, she saw that tears shone in his eyes. "I am not, I fear," he told her. "But neither am I vindictive. I wished for revenge, and now, I think you will agree, I have exacted a revenge more complete than I could ever have envisaged."

Aurora considered. "I still believe Celia should be punished."

"She has already been sorely tried by the death of her beloved brother," he reminded her. "Further punishment we may leave, I think, to God."

Still unconvinced, but seeing his decision was irrefutable, Aurora reached out. Gently, doing her best not to hurt his shoulder, she took his face between her hands. "Very well, no word of this shall pass my lips."

He nodded, his eyes closing. Tears slid from under his eyelids; Aurora wiped them with her handkerchief as if he were a child, and they did not speak again.

She sat by the bedside in the candlelight until his breathing deepened and he slept, his ill-kempt hair like an irregular stain on the pillow. Softly, she drew her finger over his jaw. It felt scratchy. Attending the barber had not been possible for several mornings past. Aurora's heart was moved as she wondered how long it would be before Edward would be able to resume the life that had been so cruelly taken from him when his adoptive father died. She pictured his fathomless eyes with their hollow, haunted expression. "Dear God," she whispered, "I pray that before many more days have passed, I will see joy upon his face."

Sleep was not possible for her. The pallet the maid had left for her was comfortable enough, but when she removed her gown and lay down in her chemise, her thoughts would give her no peace. She could not rid her memory of scenes from the time she had spent as Edward's wife. Her sisters' excitement, Edward's despair, her own dilemma, kind Mr Marshall and his gouty foot, Mrs Fellowes, Spring Gardens, the key which had unlocked not only the writing desk but the whole story of Honoria.

And Joe Deede.

She pondered on how strange it was that Joe's fair face hid such a villainous soul, and Edward's scholarly demeanour such a courageous one. And what did her own countenance hide? Round and round went reminders of the deceptions, falsehoods and disguise she had been obliged to practise in the name of seeing justice done. If she begged forgiveness, of her family and of God, surely they would forgive?

As she lay there listening to Edward's breathing, moonlight slanted from the half-open shutters and the sounds of the city diminished as the hour grew later. Gradually, one thought began to overcome all others in Aurora's head: when all was resolved, what would happen to her?

She had made a bargain with Edward. She had agreed to help him expose Henry Francis's murder if he would respect her virtue and annul, on the grounds of non-consummation, a marriage based upon a trick. But less than a month later, everything had changed.

Her fate, she realized, was in Edward's hands. This slightly built, sorrowful, bookish man had revealed himself to be the very man of action who had for so long filled her dreams. A man who rode a horse and wielded a sword, seamlessly slipping in and out of his roles as a consumptive, a Spring Gardens swaggerer, a defender of his father, his friend, his wife and now his sister. The indignation and compassion his story had aroused in her had increased when she saw the gentlemanly way he conducted himself and as she came to know his modesty and courage. But what she felt now was no longer indignation or compassion. It was as if Edward Francis had the power to work magic upon her heart.

How would she confess to him that she had changed her mind about the annulment of their marriage? And how would she bear it if his response was not the one she sought?

"Heavenly Father, forgive me!" cried out Edward suddenly. "I killed him! My dear Lord, I killed my brother!"

Though he was still not fully awakened from his dream, Edward was trying to sit up. Aurora threw back her blankets and went to his side. "It is all right, you are safe. You are safe, Edward. It is I, Aurora."

His eyes were open, but saw nothing. His head slumped against Aurora's breast. "Josiah Deede," he said, more calmly. "I wish to see Josiah Deede."

"I am persuaded he wishes to see you too," Aurora assured him. She sighed, imagining the unsettling, unpredictable meeting that must take place. "But now, try to go back to sleep. Tomorrow morning, I will send for him."

A Sovereign in Her Palm

Aurora helped Edward into one of Richard's clean shirts. He made no sound, but his teeth were set into a grimace throughout. The bandage Aurora had made by tearing her cotton underskirt into strips had done its work, and no blood yet seeped through it. But he was not out of danger; she knew she must watch every minute for signs of fever.

For now, his face felt cool enough, and the perspiration on his forehead was produced only by the struggle to change his garment. Although his eyes still held something of the disconnected look of shock, they were clear. "How do I look?" he asked her. "Fit to be presented to ..." – he gave her a quizzical look – "my father?"

"You look as you always do," said Aurora. "A little paler, perhaps."

"Then let him come up."

Aurora went to call the servant, but turned when Edward spoke again. He looked at her, resolute, but still wary. "All may be well, Aurora," he said softly.

"Aye, we must pray so."

When Josiah Deede was shown in, he removed his hat

and approached Aurora, his hand outstretched. "Good day, madam. Are you well?"

She shook his hand, noting the apprehension in his eyes, and, not for the first time, their impenetrable blackness. "Good day to you, sir," she replied. "I am well, and I am glad to see you are recovered from your indisposition."

Josiah nodded, his nervousness unabated. "I thank you, Mrs Francis." Recognition and relief flickered in Josiah's eyes as his gaze fell on Edward. He could see that his son was too badly injured to shake hands, so he gripped his hat brim with both hands and bowed stiffly. "Good day to you, sir," he said.

Edward had not taken his eyes from his father's face. He did not speak.

A tight feeling took hold of Aurora's midriff as she sat down on the chair by the bed. Her fingers again closed around the glass phial, hidden in the folds of her skirt. Celia must surely know by now that it was missing, and very likely suspected Aurora had taken it. "Mr Deede," she began, "Edward asked to see you, but he is not strong, and this visit must be brief." She indicated the bench that stood against the wall. "Please sit down."

"Thank you, I prefer to stand." He planted his feet with his back to the fireplace, his deep-set eyes fixed upon Edward's shoulder. "I am most humbly thankful that you wished to see me…" He paused, swallowing. "The more so now I see your injury is severe, Mr Francis."

"Please address me by my first name, sir," said Edward, who had to lean sideways against his pillows in order to avoid pressure on his upper arm. "I am in some discomfort, but as the matters I have to discuss with you are of great import, I could not forbear a moment longer."

Josiah nodded. To Aurora's dismay, his gaze fell on the sword-belt that rested against the wall, where Richard had left it. "Is that … the weapon?" he asked. Before Edward could speak, he added, "You must be skilled in wielding it. Joe was a more accomplished swordsman than most."

Edward's unease was clear. "My father – that is, my adoptive father – taught me well," he began. He stopped, drew breath and went on. "There is a good long hall at Marshcote, as perhaps you are aware. We fenced up and down it on many afternoons when I was a boy. By the time I was fifteen, and my father's rheumatism had overtaken him, I could take on most challengers. For sport, of course."

He did not look at Aurora. He had never mentioned his fencing prowess before; indeed, he had denied it. In a rush of astonishment she understood why. If she had been aware of his skill, would she have cherished the hope that he might be the victor in the duel? Was that a worse torment than her conviction that without divine help, he would certainly die? Edward had clearly thought so, and perhaps he was right.

"I see," said Josiah, sighing deeply. "I must offer you my most profound apologies, Edward, for what has happened in the past. I hope that you can find it in your heart to forgive me."

Edward regarded his father with steady eyes and spoke with a steady voice. "Sir," he began, "I can barely imagine the pain and grief this affair has caused you. As a gentleman and a Christian, I forgive you."

Josiah bowed his head. "I thank you, as I thank God,"

he murmured, his voice muffled by the frilled jabot he wore at his throat.

"But what I am about to say will perhaps bring you some comfort," continued Edward.

Josiah looked up. He was frowning slightly. Aurora wondered what was in Edward's mind.

"When he was mortally wounded," said Edward, "Joe struggled to say the word 'Honoria' loud enough, and more than once, so that it would be plainly heard."

"Yes?" asked his father, still unsure of Edward's meaning.

"I am convinced, sir, that as he lay dying, Joe wished the story of Honoria to come out, so that we might be reconciled, you and I. Saying her name was a way of confessing his sins, according to your religion. He could not carry the burden of hatred and revenge as he went to meet his Maker."

Josiah was gazing intently at his son. His eyes contained the mixture of darkness and brightness Aurora had so often seen in Edward's own eyes. Beneath the bluff demeanour Josiah usually wore, and the contrite apprehension he had shown this morning, Aurora knew there lay an honourable, if misguided, man. Edward's desire to spare him the final piece of the story, concerning the phial of poison, had been right. His battered heart would never have withstood it.

The effort of speaking had whitened Edward's face, especially around his lips. Aurora knew he had begun to bleed through his bandage. "We know you are innocent in this matter, sir," she assured Josiah gently. "Your sins are those of envy, intolerance and hatred, which you admit yourself. God will forgive you those, since you show true penance."

Josiah's eyes lingered upon her face for a moment, then he seemed to make a decision. "I will go to my attorney immediately. The matter of the inheritance must be settled. You may be assured," he said, nodding towards Edward, "that not only will your own estate be returned, but I intend to bequeath a good portion of my own to you, having made very good provision for my daughter."

"No!"

Edward's protest was so unexpected that Aurora jumped. She and Josiah both looked at him in surprise.

"Thank you, sir," he said to his father, "but I will accept no part of the Deede fortune. Let my own be returned to me, and I will be satisfied. I do not want your money, sir."

Bewilderment crossed Josiah's face, but he checked it. He put on his hat and made a low bow. "Very well, Edward, I will do as you say. You are more Henry's son than mine, I see."

"Thank you, sir," said Edward. His voice was weak; he would soon sleep again.

Josiah went towards the door. "Fare you well, both of you," he said. "If you should need a physician, or if there is anything I can do…"

"I will send for you," Aurora reassured him, curtseying. "He must rest now."

Josiah nodded and took hold of the latch. But when he opened the door an unexpected noise assailed Aurora's ears. The shrill keening of a distressed female rang throughout the upper floor of the inn. Layered within it was the equally loud rumble of a man's protests. Aurora could not make out their words, but sensed the panic in them. She picked up her skirts and followed Josiah out onto the landing.

Missy, Celia's maid, was sprawled across the floorboards as if she had fallen there from a great height. Harrison, greatly agitated, repeatedly tried to raise her to her feet.

"For pity's sake, Harrison, what is the matter?" demanded Josiah.

Missy was wailing now, a sodden handkerchief held to her streaming eyes. There was no interruption to her anguish.

"'Tis Miss Celia," said Harrison curtly. "She's gone. Run away."

These words inspired more vigorous sobbing from Missy. Josiah leaned against the banister post, his brow in the crook of his elbow. "Dear God, dear God," Aurora heard him murmuring. She advanced across the landing and placed her hand upon his arm. Beneath his coat sleeve he trembled uncontrollably. Fate had inflicted all it could upon the man; he was almost broken. "Mrs Francis," he gasped. "Mrs Francis—"

"Aurora," said Aurora. "Please call me Aurora."

He raised his head. His hat and wig were askew, and tears covered his cheeks. "My daughter, my darling Celia…" He strove to control himself before his man-servant, but in vain. His sobs were loud and heartfelt. "Why has she forsaken me?"

Aurora wondered the same thing. It seemed a cruel desertion of her father. But Celia *was* cruel. By now she would have missed the phial and decided to flee rather than face the consequences of its discovery. Edward had refused to confront her, but she had instead brought her own punishment upon herself. Where would she go, and how would she live?

"I cannot say, sir," she told Josiah. "But perhaps she can be found." She crouched down beside Missy. "Did your mistress hint where she might be going?"

Missy gulped back tears. "No, 'm. She never spoke to me. It … it was in my apron pocket when I put it on, and I never, I never—"

"What was in your apron pocket?" asked Aurora.

"This note, Miss," said Harrison. He held up a folded paper. "The girl gave it to me to read for her, as she weren't never taught her letters."

Aurora took the paper. "Missy, will you allow me to see what Miss Celia wrote?"

Missy nodded, too miserable to care, and Aurora unfolded the note.

Dearest Missy,

I am very sorry to leave you, but I cannot stay in this house. I am going far away. Do not try to follow me; you will never find me. Mr Harrison will attend to your references. You and your sisters may have all the clothes I have left in my closet.

Yours,

Celia Deede

Aurora gave the note back to Missy. The girl had calmed somewhat. Her small face, blotched by misery, touched Aurora. She wondered how long the girl had been Celia's maid. Whether her mistress's whereabouts became known or not, she would, she decided suddenly, keep Missy as her own personal maid. "Do not worry, Missy," she told her. "All will be well."

Aurora stood up and went to Josiah. His forehead was

deeply lined, the corners of his mouth drawn downwards. His eyes held such unspeakable despair that Aurora could hardly bear to look at him. "Sir," she said gently, "this is very distressing, but it seems Celia has, indeed, run away."

He was not listening. "My daughter must have known what her brother was about," he said grimly. "She fears her own guilt will be discovered." Seemingly unaware that both servants were staring at him, uncomprehending, he went on. "But she will be punished, you may be sure. I will not rest in my search for her, and when I find her, I will place her in a convent for the rest of her days."

Aurora could think of no answer. She pressed her father-in-law's arm, then she turned to Harrison. "Make sure your master returns home safely, and stay by his side until he is recovered." She bent to the maid, who was still sitting on the floor. "And, Missy, you may give notice to Mr Deede. I will come and bring you away, and you can be my maid instead. Would you like that?"

"Yes, 'm," whispered the girl. "Thank you, 'm."

"Sir," said Aurora to Josiah, "I will call tomorrow, but now I must attend to Edward. I bid you farewell. Go now with Harrison, I pray you, and lean on him."

When Aurora returned to Edward's room she saw that his white face was taking on a grey tinge. His jaw had stiffened against the onslaught of pain, and the animation had gone from his eyes. "Celia has admitted her own guilt by running away," she told him. "Now I must dress that wound and you must sleep."

"Where do you think Celia has bolted to?"

"I cannot imagine," replied Aurora. "Though as she once told me, she has hundreds of friends. Someone will hide her." She regarded her husband pensively. "And, as we well know, in this city anyone – even a young girl with nothing but her wits to protect her – can pretend to be someone else, and no one is any the wiser."

"Why, Mr Drayton! And your pretty sister!" Samuel Marshall approached from the back of the shop. "I had begun to wonder if I would ever see you again!"

Edward made an awkward bow, not out of embarrassment, but because his bandaged shoulder restricted his movements, and he was loath to betray his injury to Mr Marshall. "We were detained at the Black Swan for a few days," he explained. "But now we are come back, and we are pleased to see you well, sir."

Aurora dropped a curtsey. "Tell me, Mr Marshall, is Mary in the house? I must speak to her."

"Aye, and William," replied Mr Marshall, returning to his chair. "The lock on your door is replaced, and Mary has the new keys. Shall I see you later, Mr Drayton, for a glass of port?"

"Thank you, sir," said Edward politely, "but I am afraid it will not be possible to accept your invitation. My sister and I have a visit to make to Westminster, and may not return until late."

"Tomorrow, then!" said Mr Marshall, with a wave of his hand.

"Indeed." Edward gave Aurora a glance that told her to remain silent. Tomorrow, when all had been revealed to Mrs Eversedge and her daughters, they would tell Mr Marshall the truth. Today, they must still be Mr Drayton and his pretty sister.

"I am glad you are come back!" called Mr Marshall as they left the shop.

"Until tomorrow!" returned Aurora. Then, softly, to Edward, "How I hate deceiving him!"

"Then thank the Lord we do not have to do it for much longer," he said, unlocking the street door.

Mary emerged from the kitchen, her plate-like face more animated than Aurora had ever seen it. "Miss Drayton! And Mr Drayton, sir!" she exclaimed, curtseying.

Aurora had been touched by the actions, and the discretion, of this good-hearted girl. "Thank you, Mary," she said, "for helping me when I was hurt, and so distressed."

Flushing, Mary bobbed several curtseys. "You better now, Miss?"

"Much better." She turned to Edward. "And my brother also has reason to thank you."

"You did right, Mary," said Edward, "to keep what happened on Sunday and Monday to yourself, and to tell only Mr Marshall where Miss Drayton had gone. It was very important that certain people did not know. Now that there is a new lock, we may return."

Still red-faced, Mary fumbled under her apron and produced two keys. She proffered them to Edward, who took them with a smile. "Thank you," he said. With his good arm he reached into the pocket of his waistcoat. "And here is something for you. Hold out your hand."

He placed a sovereign in her palm. She stared at it with such astonishment Aurora wondered if she had ever held one before. "Do not tell William," said Edward, "or he will want one."

"Oh, sir…" Mary's small powers of speech failed her, and she ran back into the kitchen, her apron at her eyes.

"You know that she is in love with you, do you not?" asked Aurora as they climbed the stairs.

"Of course."

"You are very sure of yourself."

"I am a man of means," he said, with such satisfaction that Aurora laughed aloud. "And have every reason to be sure of myself. Now, will this key work, I wonder?"

"If it does not, you may use the skeleton key," joked Aurora.

"Do not remind me."

The key worked; the door swung open to reveal a swept, tidied room, the bed made, the table clear. Edward's trunk stood at the foot of his bed. New candles filled the holders, and the window had been cleaned. Aurora opened the inner door. The same neatness and cleanliness met her. "Bless the girl," she said. "She can be a good servant when she wants to be."

Edward laughed. "And she did this before I gave her that sovereign!" He took off his wig, threw it on the bed and opened his trunk. "I must make myself look presentable to meet your sisters," he said. "They are severe critics of male attire, I would imagine."

Aurora hesitated, but could not allow the opportunity to pass. "They are *your* sisters, too, you know."

He was sitting on the bed, rummaging one-armed in the trunk. "For the time being," he said, without looking up at her.

Boldly, she sat beside him. "I must change out of this." She indicated her creased and dirtied silk gown. "I have been wearing it since Monday evening, when Mary helped me into it. It is astonishing, is it not, that almost three days have passed since then, and I have not yet taken it off? Today is Thursday, you know."

He still did not look at her. "Very strange," he agreed. "And yes, today is Thursday."

"Edward." She edged nearer to his side. "Before I change my gown or do anything else, we must resolve our … the future."

He turned towards her at last. His face was full of serious purpose. She was reminded of the moment when he had taken hold of the tassel on Richard's bed curtain and twisted it between his fingers as if it were the most important task in the world. His hands were empty now, but instead of seizing something to concentrate on while he sought for words, he took Aurora's hand, and kissed it.

As she looked at his bent head, she was struck by the simplicity of his quickly scissored hair, which stuck up in little tufts on the crown of his head, as unregarded as that of a boy. She felt the softness of his lips upon the back of her hand, and then, when he closed his eyes and laid her palm against his cheek, the scratchiness of his unshaven skin.

She had seen Edward as many things, in many moods and many guises. But above all, he was a man who had placed himself in danger not merely for honour, but for love. She caressed his face as she spoke. "Edward, we made a bargain. You agreed not to—"

"Importune you for any favours due to a husband," he recited. "Your exact words. I remember them well."

Aurora remembered them too, with shame. What a prim little vixen she must have seemed! "And I agreed to help you expose the truth about your father's death and your disinheritance," she said. "We agreed that one month from that day, which will be the twenty-ninth of this month, seventeen days from now, we would…" She withdrew her hand. She could not speak while she was touching him; the sensation it produced rendered coherent thought impossible.

"We would part," he supplied. "With or without fortune."

Aurora said nothing. He had opened his eyes and was regarding her with such tenderness, yet with such a dream-like intensity, her heart had leapt into her throat.

"When matters became more dangerous than I had anticipated, I offered to set you free," he said, his voice as gentle, yet purposeful, as his expression. "Yet you refused. You said you had made a bargain and you would keep it. It was then that I allowed myself some small glimmer of hope that you might care more for me than for my money."

"Oh, Edward…" Gingerly, fearing to hurt him, Aurora laid her head upon his uninjured shoulder. "I cared about the injustice that had been done to you, it is true, and wished to see right done. But I also wanted the freedom to live as I wished, which only a married woman has, and although I was shocked when you revealed that you were not ill, I was thankful too."

He slid his arm around her waist. She was sure he was in pain, but she could not bear – any more than he could – to forego this makeshift embrace. "So my plainness and thinness did not thoroughly repulse you, then?" he asked.

"Repulse? No. If I am truthful, I will confess that I was disappointed, not only in your appearance, but in your avowal that you did not follow country pursuits or go into society. But you must remember that I was comparing you to an invisible man. And I had not the imagination to understand that an educated man can be many things, not merely what he presents to an ignorant girl."

"You were never an ignorant girl, Aurora. Your father and mother saw to that."

"I was not far from it. But I hope I have learned some severe lessons, and will not judge by appearances quite so readily in future."

The name of Joe Deede hovered between them, but neither spoke it. Aurora gazed at Edward, wondering how her tight-lipped, indignant bargain had become this unshakeable desire never to be parted from him again. She already knew he could do magic, but here surely was alchemy, transforming not metal into gold, but indifference into love.

"May I hope, then," asked Edward, his lips so close she could feel his breath on her cheek, "for the happiness that making you my true wife would bring me?"

Aurora smiled. "You may hope, indeed, that your wound heals well, and you are soon able to give your wife the embraces she longs for."

He had kissed her lips before, at their wedding, when she still expected to be his "true wife". But when he kissed them now it was with a different kind of kiss, the joy of which came from deep within him, and surprised her with its passion. She found herself returning it with equal passion, hoping he felt her own joy, and willing God to prolong the moment. To return the love of a man who had never wavered in his love of her was surely the most perfect union two people could have on earth.

"We shall have our marriage blessed, in the sight of God, before many more weeks have passed," promised Edward as they drew apart. "At St Margaret's."

"I care not where, as long as you are by my side," said Aurora, trying to conceal the flush that had risen into her cheeks. What need had she to colour? This man was her husband. And yet, as they both knew, she was not yet his true wife.

It was as if he had read her thoughts. He took his arm from around her waist and regarded her solemnly, though with an immodest gleam in his eyes. "But before that, my dearest Aurora, sword wound or no, you shall be mine." He glanced at the door. "I did lock it, did I not?"

Mrs Eversedge's small sofa was in its usual place, the worked cushions still covered the window seats and the straight-backed chairs, and the gap at the top of the half-closed shutter where it had slipped on its hinge still revealed a thin slice of the brightness outside. But this familiar room, the room where Edward had made his extraordinary proposal, now gleamed with more than sunlight. Aurora's mother and sisters at last knew the truth, and once their astonishment had been tempered, they embraced her and her husband with more happiness than the parlour had ever contained.

"A house in Lincolnshire!" exclaimed Mrs Eversedge. "With a park, for riding! Girls, imagine!"

Edward smiled. "I am not much of a horseman, but—"

"Yes, he is," interrupted Aurora. "He said he was not much of a swordsman, and that was a downright lie, so you may be assured that he is the best horseman in the whole of Lincolnshire."

Flora waited for the laughter that followed this to subside, then she said, "I simply cannot believe such a thing can happen! And it all began that day in the park when we saw Edward and that other man!" She threw a look at Edward, her round face aglow with delight. "I can say this now because you are my much-beloved brother, but my sisters and I agreed that day that your companion was both taller and fairer than you. How disappointed we were that it turned out to be *you* that was interested in pursuing Aurora! That other man was only watching her."

Aurora looked at Edward, who was watching Flora keenly. "You are speaking of Richard, are you not?" he asked her.

Flora's smile faltered; her glance slid to Aurora, then back to Edward. "Well, Richard is tall and fair, and when I saw him at the wedding I thought I might as well flirt with him a little. He may have been with you in the park, but I do not remember him there. I mean the man standing near you at the gate, a little behind you, as I recall." She stopped, puzzled. "Why are you looking at me like that? I have not offended you, have I?"

"No, my dear Flora," said Edward hurriedly. "Do you remember enough of this man's looks to describe them more fully?"

Flora tapped her chin with her finger, happy to be the centre of attention. "He wore a suit like any other man, and a wig... Oh! I believe his coat cuffs were decorated with a great deal of gold. I remember how they glinted when he raised his arm to shield his eyes from the sun. I thought he must be very rich. And his hat was very fine, with white plumes."

"Good God," said Edward blankly, "Joe Deede."

"He must have been following you," said Aurora. "He knew from the start that you were suspicious of your father's actions. That day in the park, he saw you looking at us, and watched you and Richard follow us out of the park gates. So when he saw me at the Theatre Royal, he had his sister intercept Mrs Fellowes so he could meet me. Not because he thought I was beautiful, as he said, but because he wanted to find out if I was up to mischief."

"Hah!" interjected Flora. "All the time you thought you were deceiving him, he was deceiving you! How funny!"

"It is not funny, you *child*," scolded Eleanora. "Aurora was in danger. This is the man who murdered Edward's father and tried to murder Edward too, remember? I think she is lucky to have escaped with her life. Do you not agree, Edward?"

"Indeed," said Edward. "But the danger is over now."

"Unless Celia Deede decides to return with another phial of poison," said Eleanora, who had been most fascinated by this part of the story.

"She will not," Edward assured her. "She has nothing to gain by it."

"Except revenge on you for her brother's death," said Aurora, who had also pondered on this. "She loved him every bit as dearly as I love my sisters."

Edward nodded. "We will be on our guard. The case against Celia will never be tried in court – her flight is an admission of guilt, but there is no proof that Henry

Francis was poisoned, or that she administered the poison. However, if she comes within ten miles of her father you may be confident he will put her in the convent and turn the key on her for ever."

"Then let that be the end of it," said Mrs Eversedge. An ever-vigilant hostess, she stood up and indicated for Aurora to lead the way out of the room. "A cold collation awaits us downstairs," she announced. "Roast beef, pies, fresh baked bread, cheese, jellies, sweetmeats, everything. Now, let us have no more talk of crime and punishment, but eat with our hearts at rest. Everything turned out well in the end, though if I had known about it, I swear I would have died myself, of anxiety."

"I could not tell you, though I longed to," confessed Aurora.

"Dearest girl!" said Mrs Eversedge with affection. "You are so thoughtful, and very worthy of your husband's love."

Flora caught Aurora up, and whispered to her as they entered the dining room. "Speaking of husbands, Richard is not the man I saw in the park, to be sure. But that is not to say he is any less handsome than the man I *did* see. And you know, now I look at Edward more closely, my dear Aurora, and know that he is a skilled horseman and can wield a sword, I consider him quite the hero!"

Aurora took her sister's arm. "He *is* a hero," she said. "But his heroism has nothing to do with a horse or a sword."

Flora frowned. "You do say some odd things sometimes, Aurora," she said accusingly. "I do not understand you."

Aurora thought how strange and wonderful it was that her disappointment at her first sight of Edward had become in so few weeks an unbreakable bond. Her feelings had twisted their way through fear, suspicion, horror, triumph, sorrow, compassion and, finally, affection. They had met crossroads and blind alleys; she had taken wrong turnings. But now a clear road lay ahead of her and her dearest Edward, for ever.

"You will," she said, squeezing her sister's arm, "when you fall in love."

Author biography

Vice and Virtue is the latest addition to Veronica Bennett's list of historical novels (*Angelmonster*, based on the life of Mary Shelley; *Cassandra's Sister*, about the young Jane Austen; and *Shakespeare's Apprentice*). Inspiration for its heroine, Aurora, came from Sarah Egerton (1670–1723). "Sarah," explains Veronica, "was an early champion of feminine independence, publishing a feminist pamphlet at the age of sixteen. Extraordinarily, only a year later, she entered into an arranged marriage with a man ten years older than herself. In view of her condemnation of society's treatment of women, we can only ask … why?"

Veronica Bennett was an English lecturer for several years but now writes full-time. In 2011 she was elected a Hawthornden Fellow. She is married to a university professor and has two adult children.

Cassandra's Sister by Veronica Bennett

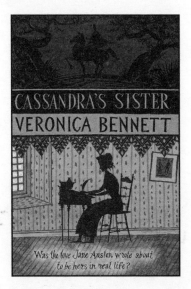

Young Jane – or Jenny, as she was known – is a girl with
a head full of questions that no one seems able to answer.
But the sudden arrival of her worldly wise cousin, Eliza,
to the parsonage in rural Hampshire brings Jenny some
of the answers she is seeking and provides the germ of
an idea... Building on the close relationship between
Jane and her older sister, Cassandra, and drawing on
characters and incidents from such masterpieces as *Pride
and Prejudice* and *Sense and Sensibility*, *Cassandra's Sister*
creates a moving portrait of one of the world's greatest
and best-loved writers.

*A powerful, fictionalized account of how love, death and
betrayal shaped the life of novelist Jane Austen*